Not
AR

FUTURE FRIGHT
TALES OF HIGH-TECH TERROR

by Don Wulffson

Lowell House
Juvenile
Los Angeles

CONTEMPORARY BOOKS
Chicago

For my good friend Tom Tarter,
whose "memories of the dead" were clearer than my own.

—D.W.

Cover illustration by Scott Fray

Library of Congress Catalog Card Number: 96-138
ISBN: 1-56565-393-9

Publisher: Jack Artenstein
General Manager, Juvenile Division: Elizabeth Amos
Director of Publishing Services: Rena Copperman
Editor-in-Chief, Juvenile Fiction: Barbara Schoichet
Managing Editor, Juvenile Division: Lindsey Hay
Art Director: Lisa-Theresa Lenthall
Typesetting: Jim Storck

Lowell House books can be purchased at special discounts when ordered in bulk for
premiums and special sales. Contact Department JH at the following address:

Lowell House Juvenile
2029 Century Park East, Suite 3290
Los Angeles, CA 90067

Manufactured in the United States of America
10 9 8 7 6 5 4 3 2 1

CONTENTS

IMMORTALITY
5

PERFECT LITTLE SWEETHEARTS
25

INNER EYES
43

MEMORIES OF THE DEAD
57

THE SCREAMING OF THE TREES
69

FUTURE CALLER
83

IMMORTALITY

The book contained pictures of bodies—dead bodies with flaky-looking skin and rotting sores. Fifteen-year-old Chadwick Moore found the pictures fascinating. He looked up from the book. "You were alive at the time of the Bulbar Plague of 2072, weren't you, Joseph?" Chadwick asked the servant, who was quietly electro-mopping the already spotless marble floor of Chadwick's bedroom.

"Yes, Master Moore," said Joseph, looking over wearily at the boy he'd served for the past decade and a half.

"What was it like?" Chadwick asked, wonder in his eyes.

"Quite awful, sir," Joseph said, furrowing his brow.

"It says in this book that over eighty-seven percent of the population of the world died as a result of that plague," Chadwick went on, running a hand through his blue-tinted hair. "How did they dispose of all the bodies?" He grinned mischievously. "I already read about it, but I want you to tell me, anyway."

Joseph sighed. His master loved to waste his time and annoy him. "Many were burned or buried. Many were dumped in the sea. Others just lay in the streets and rotted."

"Can you read, Joseph?" Chadwick asked, knowing the answer to that as well.

"No, sir," the old man replied in a monotone. "I've had no formal schooling. All I know of this life is what I've seen of it."

"Pity you can't read," Chadwick said haughtily. "Some of the most recent findings as to the cause of the plague are quite intriguing. The viral mold was released by a rather small and seemingly insignificant earthquake in a place once known as Pakistan. Have you ever heard of Pakistan, Joseph?"

"No, sir," said the old man, his faded blue eyes staring at the boy.

"Well, it was there that the plague originated. It killed everyone without a B-Positive blood type." Chadwick arched a brow. "Do you know what blood-typing is, Joseph?"

"No, sir."

"It seems, Joseph," said Chadwick, "that you don't know much at all. In fact, you're terribly ignorant. Do you agree?"

"Yes, Master Moore."

"I'm glad you do," said Chadwick. "Because if you had disagreed, I would have had to report you to the Conduct Committee and have you disposed of. As it is, I've been pondering your fate."

Joseph stiffened.

"You're getting to be quite old, Joseph—fifty-eight, according to government records. And you've become slow and inefficient. Fact is, I'm not sure what purpose your continued presence on this earth serves. I'll be deciding within the next week whether or not to contact the Euthanasia Council about having you put down."

Joseph said nothing and did nothing. He knew he was being goaded, and fully aware of what the consequences would be to any sort of outburst.

Keep your mouth shut, Joseph, he told himself. *The little snoot can nail you for misconduct. But you're not sixty yet, old man, and until you reach legal death-age, even his little highness over there can't pull enough strings to have you butchered.*

"Please get back to work now," said Chadwick Moore, smirking slightly. "I'm through talking to you."

Joseph nodded and turned on the electro-mop. But when he saw Chadwick's finger wagging at him, he turned it off again. "You wanted something else, sir?"

"Yes, one more thing," said Chadwick. "I'll be meeting Mother for supper at Le Fontaine's at eight, and from there we'll proceed to ICON Labs. Rather than take a Slide-Taxi, I think I'd prefer a ride in a classic internal-combustion automobile. Please see to it that a vehicle and driver are ready to deliver me."

"Very well, sir," said Joseph. "I'll see to it immediately."

He was glad that the cruel, spoiled boy hadn't opted for the same mode of transportation as last time—by rickshaw. Joseph's feet still had sores on them from that twenty kilometer trek.

At Le Fontaine's, while waiting for their meal to be served, Chadwick and his mother began to argue.

"Sometimes, Chadwick," said his mom, running a hand through her short-cropped pink-tinted hair, "I don't think you fully realize how lucky you are. Until Nascent City was built in 2057, no one—and I mean *no one*—had anything. I'm telling you, people were so hungry they would kill for a piece of—"

"For a piece of bread," Chadwick interrupted with a yawn.

"What I'm getting at, dear, is that although things are better now, and at least most people have a constant food supply, we still live in a very elitist society. Do you know how hard I worked to get us inside The Walls?" his mother asked. "Do you know what's *outside*? Well, let me tell you, while we lucky few sit here, guarded around the clock, most of the population lives in squalor." She shook her head. "Only a few strong ones are allowed in to serve us. We must treat them with compassion."

"But my teachers told me that we got behind The Walls and into Nascent City because we're of higher intelligence and breeding," replied Chadwick.

"Your teachers only tell you what they're allowed to tell you," his mother replied.

"Maybe," said Chadwick, "but those who live inside The Walls are the scientists, doctors, and government officials who make society work. I mean, the reason *we're* inside The Walls is because you're the director of gerontology for ICON."

"Well, to a certain extent you're right," said his mother, candlelight playing across her face in the dimly lit restaurant. "But I worry about your attitude toward those less fortunate than yourself. Last week you were seen throwing stones at workers and slaves down at the construction site of the new high-rise buildings. And yesterday you were overheard bragging in class that you could have Joseph killed if you wanted to."

"Well, I *can*, at least as soon as the council lowers the death-age for servants to 55."

"The Proviso hasn't been approved yet," his mother replied. "And anyway, why would you want Joseph put down? He's been a good servant, hasn't he?"

"I treat Joseph well," snapped Chadwick, ignoring her question. "I treat him almost as an equal. I even *talk* to him!"

"Yes, and that's good of you, but—"

"I'm nicer to Joseph than most people are to their servants and slaves," Chadwick went on. "I really am, and I don't know why you say I'm not!"

"Don't get upset, dear," his mother said, trying to keep her voice calm and steady. She was totally unaware that, inside, Chadwick was laughing, while outside his face bore a look of a totally misunderstood and very innocent boy. In fact, at that very moment, Chadwick was concentrating with all his might, trying to force a single tear from his eye. He succeeded.

"Oh, dear!" his mother exclaimed. "You *are* upset, aren't you?" And with that she began nervously plowing through her purse for a handkerchief.

Meanwhile, with his mother's attention diverted, Chadwick quickly stuck his leg out in front of a boy waiter-slave who was passing by their table. Instantly the boy went flying—as did the tray of food he had been carrying. One angry diner, his purple hair wet with soup, got up and kicked the boy in a rage. And momentarily the young waiter was set upon by the management. After pummeling him with their fists, they dragged him out the door and threw him into the street. He crawled a few feet away, then collapsed.

The manager, himself a part of the servant class, came over and nervously began apologizing profusely to the angry, food-besmirched customers.

"I'm turning in you and your whole staff to the Conduct Council!" snarled a woman dabbing at her ruined gown.

Chadwick and his mother, already up from their seats, watched as long as they could bear it. Finally, distressed by the entire scene and not knowing what else to do, they made their way out of the restaurant.

"Do you want to go home?" Chadwick's mother asked him. "Or shall we go somewhere else to eat?"

"No, Mom," said Chadwick, still pretending to be horrified by what had just transpired, when actually he'd not only caused the scene but had totally enjoyed it. "I'm not hungry, but let's still go over to ICON as we'd planned." He mustered a smile. "I don't want the whole evening going to waste. You've been excited for weeks while hinting there was something special you were going to show me at the lab tonight. So let's just forget about everything else and go to ICON, okay?"

"Lead the way, Master," his mother said with a smile, then chuckled at her little joke.

Their driver, waiting by the car Chadwick had ordered, opened the door for them as the two approached. As they were about to duck into the backseat, Chadwick's mother gasped and pointed at the hapless waiter-slave who'd just been thrown out of the restaurant. He was limping down the street, trying to get away from police officers who were now descending on him from every direction. Within seconds they electrocuted him on the spot with a Sparkgun.

"How terrible," said Chadwick's mother after the two of them had gotten into the automobile.

Chadwick turned and looked out the back window as the car pulled away. "Yes, Mother, it really is," he said, feeling no emotion other than pleasure for having caused the boy's death. His one regret was that his shin hurt a little, but it had been worth it. In fact, all the way to ICON he was chuckling inside.

Although ICON was shut down for the night, the security guards greeted the director of gerontology and her son warmly, then escorted them to her private office.

As soon as the guards left, Chadwick's mom pulled a lock-wand from her purse and depressed the thumb control. A blue light spewed forth and the far office wall faded away, revealing a large laboratory.

"Fantastic!" exclaimed Chadwick, following his mother inside. "I didn't even know this laboratory existed!"

"Not many people do," his mother said, enjoying her son's enthusiastic response.

Chadwick walked around gazing at everything with wonderment. The lab was a maze of scientific paraphernalia along with cages full of animals and translucent canisters full of bugs, worms, and insects.

"Pretty soon I'll be going public with my work," his mother said excitedly. "Gerontology is the study of aging, as you know. But I've been doing more than just researching how and why people get old. I'm on to something *very* exciting, Chadwick, and I wanted you to be the first to see what I've finally discovered after all these years."

"What?" asked Chadwick, his eyes wide with excitement.

"Well, it has to do with Telomerase," his mother began. "That's something that controls aging and mortality."

"Don't tell me you've discovered the key to eternal life?" Chadwick gasped.

His mother nodded, grinning from ear to ear. "Yes, Chadwick. I've discovered the key to immortality!" she exclaimed, walking over to a counter and picking up a glass container with a big fat cockroach in it. "This is Mortimer, and he's going to live forever." She put the container down and made her way to a cage with a baby chimp in it. "And this is Vivian, my favorite subject. How old do you think she is?"

"Only a few months," Chadwick replied.

"Nope—she's five *years* old!" his mother said, beaming. "You see, I injected her with my serum as an infant, and now Vivian will live forever—*as a baby!*"

Chadwick gazed around the lab. "Are all the animals in here going to live forever?" he asked.

His mother shook her head. "Unfortunately, I don't have enough of the serum. Only Mortimer, Vivian, and Gus are immortal." She strummed her fingers on the cage of a large rat. "Gus is *never* going to die, right, big guy?" She threw the healthy looking rodent a big hunk of cheese, which it gobbled up immediately.

"But if I strangled him, for example, he'd die, wouldn't he?" asked Chadwick with a sly smile.

"Oh, I've already tried killing him," his mother replied matter-of-factly. "Starvation, poison gas, suffocation—I've tried them all, both on Mortimer and on Gus."

"You mean they *can't* be killed?" Chadwick's eyes widened in disbelief.

"Correct," his mother answered. "The serum causes the cells to readjust to any circumstances—no matter how extreme."

"Pretty amazing stuff," said Chadwick. "Can I see what the serum looks like?"

Nodding, his mother took the lock-wand from her purse once again and pointed it at what looked like a bare wall. Suddenly a wall safe appeared, then slid open. "Here it is," his mother said, removing a vial containing a jade-green liquid from the safe.

"This is all you have?" asked Chadwick.

"That's all there is," his mother said. "But it's enough for the final step."

"And that is . . . ?" Chadwick asked, already anticipating the answer.

"Human injection," his mother replied. "Within the month, a subject from the slave classes will be selected as a guinea pig for the experiment."

The next morning the body of Chadwick's mother was found lying in the courtyard of ICON Laboratories. She appeared to have fallen—or been pushed—from several stories up. A potted plant had also fallen, and investigators quickly determined that it had come from the balcony outside her office. Examination of the balcony showed signs of a struggle—a small table had been knocked over and a French door had been shattered.

Police questioned security guards about the incident, and two officers sped to the woman's home to speak to her son. Only Joseph was there.

"Master Chadwick and his mother did not return home as scheduled last night," Joseph told them.

After a brief search of the premises, the two police officers headed back to the station by slide-car. But on the way they were contacted by radio-phone and told to proceed immediately to Patrician Pools, Nascent City's swimming complex reserved for the highest level of The Wall residents.

Upon arriving moments later, the officers were met by a frantic pool attendant. "This way!" the man cried, running toward the large outdoor pool that was closed for the winter.

"I—I can't swim!" the attendant said feebly. "I tried to go in after him, but I—"

But the officers weren't listening. They were gazing in horror at a body lying on the bottom of the deep end of the pool. Quickly the female officer kicked off her shoes and dove into the icy water. The male officer followed her in, and moments later the two emerged from the pool, dragging the corpse of Chadwick Moore.

That afternoon a balding little man, an assistant coroner at Nascent City Morgue, pushed through the swinging doors into a marble-floored room full of neon shadows. Cold steel compartments lined the walls.

"Nine-seven-three," he mumbled to himself as he glanced from his clipboard to the numbers above the stainless steel compartments. "Ah, here we are," he said under his breath, then punched the button beside the drawer marked 917.

A lock clicked, the door opened, and a sheet-draped body lying on a long metal table rolled out. The assistant checked the tag hanging from the body's left big toe. He wrote the date and time on the death paper, then took one corner of the sheet between his forefinger and thumb and pulled it back.

"Poor kid," he muttered, looking at the bluish, puckered-skin corpse of Chadwick Moore.

And then he screamed insanely.

Chadwick Moore's eyes had flipped open. "Oh, there's nothing *poor* about me," he said, sitting up and giggling uproariously, as the horrified attendant fell unconscious to the floor.

That night Chadwick was inconsolable as he lay in a hospital bed with doctors, nurses, and two police investigators hovering around him.

"My poor mother!" he cried. "I can't believe she's gone. I'm all alone now!" And with that he broke into the most convincing wail he could muster.

"Can you tell us anything about that night?" asked a dark-haired female investigator.

"Well, after supper Mother and I went to ICON," Chadwick began tearfully. "She was showing me around her private laboratory when three security guards broke in on us. She had just opened her wall safe, and apparently those horrid guards were after whatever was in there." He dramatically brushed a tear from his cheek. "Mother and I fought them and she broke free for a moment and got as far as her office. Then something shattered—the door leading out to the balcony, I think. And after that I heard her cry out. I tried to run to her, but I just . . ." His voice trailed off. "I guess I was knocked unconscious, because I don't remember anything after that."

"Do you remember how you ended up in the pool?" asked the female officer.

Chadwick shook his head, sniffled, and gazed sadly into space. "I guess the guards threw me in and tried to drown me," he said, knitting his brow as though struggling to figure out what had happened to him.

"We don't know how long you were underwater," said one of the doctors, stepping forward, "but a minimum of ten minutes elapsed between the time you were first spotted and before you could be brought to the surface."

"It's a miracle," said another doctor. "It's truly amazing that you're still alive."

"According to the three security guards at ICON," said a male officer wearing Reflecta-Glasses, "you were seen leaving the building by a back entrance at about 9:50 P.M. They said that you told them your mother was still upstairs and did not want to be disturbed." The officer smiled. "But of course, they were lying. After all, you didn't throw *yourself* to the bottom of that pool!"

"Of course not," Chadwick said, laughing softly at such an obviously silly notion. He paused for a moment. "What's going to happen to the guards who lied?" he asked innocently.

"Oh, they've already been executed," said the officer. "And death, I might add, isn't punishment enough for their kind!"

After a week in the hospital, Chadwick was getting bored with the parade of well-wishers, doctors, and interviewers. The moment he set foot in his own house, he ordered Joseph to tell anyone coming to visit him that he was not to be disturbed. He still found pleasure in reading the news magazines about "The ICON Tragedy" and "Chadwick Moore—Miracle Boy," but the stories about the strange goings-on that night had an increasingly stale, redundant ring to them. All were mindless rehashings by government journalists who, in reality, knew nothing of what had actually occurred. But *he* knew exactly what had happened that night, and over and over again he replayed the exciting memories in his head as he lounged around "recuperating."

In his mind's eye, Chadwick saw himself snatching the vial from the safe and then running from the lab into his mother's office. Yelling, she had come after him, and they had begun grappling for the vial. In the struggle, Chadwick had almost dropped the precious serum. What a tragedy that would have been! But instead, he managed to hold on to the vial as he and his mother crashed through the French doors and out onto the balcony. Too bad his mother wasn't able to hold on to the railing. But then again, she shouldn't have rushed at him like that. Chadwick shook his head as he remembered hearing the ugly *thump* in the courtyard below, and the awkward silence that had followed.

Moments later, in the quiet of his mother's office, Chadwick had injected himself with the serum, then he'd fled down the back stairs, where he'd encountered those pesky guards. Thank goodness they were no longer a problem! While sneaking through the grounds of Patrician Pools, he'd suddenly been struck with an inspiration. It was the perfect alibi, not to mention the ultimate test of the drug! And so Chadwick Moore had indeed thrown himself into the frigid water of the outdoor pool. Then, holding his breath until he'd passed out, he'd stayed at the bottom of the pool until someone had found his very much alive—but very dead-looking—body.

A soft knock at the door startled Chadwick out of his reverie. "Enter!" he snarled, and with that, Joseph quietly walked into the room carrying a tray.

"What do *you* want?" Chadwick asked with a sneer.

"Would you care for lunch, Master?" Joseph asked, displaying an array of fruits and breads on the tray.

"No!" Chadwick snapped.

"Very well, sir," said the old man, turning to leave.

"Have the three animals I ordered from ICON arrived yet?" Chadwick asked irritably.

"Yes, Master. They arrived this morning. They're downstairs in—"

"*Downstairs?*" Chadwick screeched. "Why didn't you tell me, you ridiculous old fool?"

"I am only allowed to speak when spoken to, Master."

Chadwick glowered angrily. "Well, Joseph, fetch them immediately," he demanded. "And bring a knife!"

It was with a keen sense of anticipation that Chadwick summoned Joseph up to his room later that evening.

"Joseph, please look in this container," he said, handing the servant a sparkle-glass box. "Now tell me—what do you see?"

The old man's eyes went wide with horror as he looked inside the box.

"What do you see?" demanded Chadwick.

"I—I see a cockroach, sir," Joseph stammered.

Chadwick grinned. "What else?"

"There are many pins stuck in it," Joseph replied, revulsion on his face.

"Does it appear to be dead?" Chadwick asked casually.

"No, sir," the old man said, his eyes drifting in the direction of a cage sitting on the nightstand. He stared at what was inside with total disbelief.

"That's Gus the Rat," Chadwick said snickering. "As you can see, I've cut his head off. But incredibly, not only is his body stumbling around on its own, the head is also alive." He paused as if thinking. "My favorite part is the head. See how the eyes are looking around? It's as though the poor thing is searching for something that's been misplaced!"

Joseph, completely dumbfounded, continued to stare.

"Are you wondering why the creatures are still alive?" asked Chadwick.

"Yes, sir," Joseph managed to say. "Yes, sir, I am."

"Do you think there might be a connection between what you see now and the fact that *I* survived for many hours submerged in water?"

Joseph looked away. "I—I wouldn't know, Master."

"I think you're lying, Joseph," said Chadwick with a smirk. "In fact, I think you know more than you're willing to let on. I think that what you have just seen now, put together with what you know of my miraculous survival, would start even *your* dull brain to working."

Joseph clenched his jaw.

"Allow me to put into words what is going through your mind," Chadwick said arrogantly. "My mother, as you know, worked at ICON Laboratories, and she was there with me—her loving son—on the night that she died. But before my dear mother met her untimely death, she managed to show me her latest discovery—a serum that not only enabled me to survive for several hours at the bottom of a pool, but that also enables these two creatures that should be dead to remain alive." Chadwick threw his servant a smug smile. "Life eternal was my mother's goal, Joseph, and she achieved it."

Joseph forced himself to smile. "Your mother was a fine lady," he said.

"Indeed, and because of her, *I* am now immortal!" Chadwick exclaimed.

"I'm pleased for you, Master Moore."

Chadwick laughed. "And now do you see what I've done by sharing these secrets with you, old man? Do you see the awkward position I've put you in?"

Joseph nodded.

"I've put you in a position where you, unwittingly, have become a threat to me. You could blab things, possibly to the authorities. You could cause me problems. And I can't have that, Joseph," Chadwick said, grinning evilly. "No, I cannot. Besides, the Code of Conduct forbids it. The rules are quite clear about any servant or slave who is a threat to his master's well-being and peace of mind."

"But—" Joseph began.

"But nothing!" Chadwick screamed. "Now listen here, old man. I'm sure you're aware of the penalty for this breach of the rules." Chadwick sighed. "And what *is* that penalty, Joseph?"

The old man hung his head..

"Tell me," the boy taunted.

"The penalty is death," said Joseph, his voice little more than a whisper.

"That will be all, Joseph," said Chadwick. And with a flick of the wrist, the master dismissed his servant.

Arising early the next morning, Chadwick contemplated how he would torture Vivian, the baby chimp. Endless possibilities occurred to him, so many it was hard to make up his mind. Postponing his brutalization of the animal, he decided to take a walk.

After dressing in a lime-green silk suit, he summoned Joseph, leashed the chimp, and the three set off along one of the familiar pathways leading from his home into the pasture where new high-rises were under construction.

"I have a great deal on my mind these days," the boy told Joseph as they strolled along with Vivian hooting and hopping about playfully on the leash that Joseph held. The servant and animal had clearly grown fond of one another. "So much is changed with Mother gone. The title to the house, all monetary assets and all properties—including chattel such as yourself— have now automatically been transferred to my name."

Joseph said nothing. Instead he clacked his tongue at Vivian, who had been straining against the leash. Instantly the chimp scampered next to him, jumped up and down a couple of times, then fell right into step by his side.

"Speaking of chattel," Chadwick droned on, "I hear that there are now enough votes in the assembly to have the Servant Code changed to lower the death-age to 55. Have you heard about that, old man?"

"I heard something about it, sir," Joseph replied as they entered the construction site of a large building and began wending their way through a gridwork of concrete pylons.

"And when the death-age is lowered, all euthanasia of servants will be at the discretion of the owner," Chadwick said with a grin, "which made me start thinking of a replacement for you. And do you know what I concluded, Joseph?"

"No, sir," Joseph answered. "I don't."

"I decided that I just might be keeping you—for a little while. Not only am I terribly fond of you, but I think you could be very useful in training your replacement."

"That's good to hear, sir. I would do my best," the servant replied, his voice dripping with forced sincerity.

"To this end, I had a Safe Conduct Pass sent over to the house by messenger last night. This will allow you to leave The Walls without being harmed in order to accompany me. Out amongst the riffraff, I'll be wanting you to help in the selection of a new servant."

"Very good, sir."

Taking a plasti-card from his breast pocket, Chadwick held it out for Joseph to see. "This is the pass," he said, almost shoving it in Joseph's face. "I'll bet you're tempted to grab it. In fact, you'd probably kill me to get it, wouldn't you?"

"I had no such thought, sir."

Grinning, Chadwick put the plasti-card back into his pocket, then climbed onto a low wall that overlooked the cement gridwork below. Vivian hopped up effortlessly, followed by Joseph, who with difficulty pulled himself up, too. Wearily he sat down on the wall, then smiled at Vivian, who began busying herself by playing with the servant's hair.

"I always enjoy seeing the big skyscrapers go up," mused Chadwick, sitting down next to Joseph and gazing out at the construction site.

Below, electric hammers banged and gas-powered riveters whirred. Worker-slaves, bowed under heavy loads of concrete, trudged by. Others electro-bolted prefab concrete walls and flooring into place as soon as they were lowered into position by mammoth cranes.

Vivian ran back and forth along the wall as far as the leash would permit. Chadwick was startled when the chimp suddenly jumped into his lap.

"Get off me, you stupid beast!" Chadwick grumbled, pushing her away. "Joseph, get this animal off me!" he ordered, jumping to his feet as Vivian clung to him.

But the old man's attention was, for once, not directed on his master. It was directed on what was *above* his master.

Following Joseph's gaze, Chadwick looked up to see a great slab of prefab concrete high overhead. As he stared at the massive thing dangling from the cables of a mammoth crane, he felt a hand go into the breast pocket of his suit.

"Vivian, no!" he shrieked as the playful chimp danced away, the Safe Conduct Pass in her hand.

"Joseph, get that pass!" Chadwick bellowed.

"As you wish, sir," said Joseph. And kneeling down, he clucked his tongue at the chimp.

Instantly Vivian bounded toward the old man. She held the card out to him, then withdrew it teasingly.

"Be a good girl," said Joseph softly.

Hooting and chortling, the chimp tossed the card into the air and Joseph caught it on the fly.

"Now give it to me!" Chadwick ordered the old servant.

"With pleasure, sir!" snarled Joseph. And with a shout of triumph, he slammed his fist full force into the boy's face.

The following afternoon, Joseph, with Vivian in his arms, showed his pass to the guards at the gate, then hurried away through the squatters' camp outside The Walls. By nightfall, he and the chimp were happily making their way along a quiet country road.

Meanwhile, Chadwick Moore lay on his back, staring up into a darkness beyond perception. He remembered being hit by Joseph, and he remembered falling and striking his head, but that was all. What he didn't remember was how he had gotten wedged under the slab of concrete, or how the rest of the structure had been built on top of his body, now crushed, but very much alive.

Joseph? his mind screamed. *Mother? Anybody!!!!*

In the foundation of what would later be named Centenniel Towers, Chadwick Moore lay. The concrete floor on top of him didn't allow for even a fraction of movement. He couldn't even move his mouth to scream. As time passed Chadwick realized that in this cement coffin he could do absolutely nothing—nothing but think . . . and pray for death.

PERFECT LITTLE SWEETHEARTS

Sixteen-year-old Susan O'Casey plunked down her backpack and books on the kitchen counter. "There's something wrong with Brian," she told her parents. "He's been at that stupid boarding school since September, and he's only written once. But that's not what the problem is. It's *what* he wrote. I mean, it didn't even sound like him!"

"Rathmore is a fine school," her dad said, his head buried in the newspaper. "Your brother's in good hands. In fact, I think that school is finally turning him around."

"But why can't we ever go see him?" Susan insisted.

"Because," said her mother, who looked around the immaculate kitchen with satisfaction, then proceeded to set the breakfast table, "the teachers at Rathmore feel that, for now, Brian's contact with his family should be kept to a minimum."

"*To a minimum!*" Susan cried. "We already see Brian so little it's like he doesn't exist! I mean, he's your son—your kid! You act as though you're glad he's gone."

"We are *not* glad Brian's gone," her dad said, putting his newspaper aside neatly. "Susan, do you think this is easy for us, that we don't miss your brother and worry about him, too?"

"Well, you coulda fooled me," Susan scoffed.

"You think I like paying $19,000 a year for that school?" her father demanded, nervously straightening his tie. "Do you think I like having a son who's such a behavior problem that he can't live with us? Do you think I like that?"

"To be honest, Dad, yes. You seem to like things better the way they are now."

"I've heard just about enough of this," Susan's mother said sternly. "Your father and I are making great sacrifices so that Brian will turn out to be the kind of person we want him to be."

"*You* want!" Susan exclaimed. "How about the kind of person *he* wants to be?"

Her mother put her hands on her hips. "And what kind of person is that? A kid who flunks out of school? Who gets suspended for playing stupid pranks on his teachers? Who listens to that hideous music night and day? What should we have done? Let Brian continue to be a kid with no future, who wastes his life dreaming of—"

"Yeah, Brian *does* have dreams," Susan said. "He wants to write music and sing. Is that so bad?"

Her father glared at her. "It is when he cuts class to hang around with his low-life friends to practice that sick, negative . . ." He paused, struggling to find the right words. "I don't know what to call it, but it sure isn't *music*."

"Well, I like Brian's music!" Susan protested. "And I like—"

"That's quite enough out of you, young lady!" her father snapped, trying to control his anger. "I'm getting very tired of you talking back. You're acting just like Brian—always smart-mouthing your mother and me. I'm telling you, Susan, the way you've been behaving lately is just awful."

"No, Dad. What's awful is what you've done to Brian!" Susan shot back. "Sending him away to Rathmore—*that's* what's awful!" Furious, she snatched up her backpack, stormed from the room, then slammed the front door behind her.

After Susan's outburst, her parents did some real soul-searching. Were they doing the right thing in sending Brian to Rathmore? They really didn't know for sure. Troubled, they put in a call to the headmaster of the school, Thomas Rathmore III.

For a good hour, Mr. Rathmore patiently listened to every one of their concerns, calmly answered their questions, and skillfully put their minds at ease. In fact, after the conversation, Susan's parents not only felt reassured in their decision that Rathmore was the place for Brian, but they also felt that Thomas Rathmore III had given them some good, solid advice as to how to handle Susan's ever-increasing behavioral problems.

As for Susan, she didn't even want to come home from school that afternoon. Everybody would be tense and she'd either get the silent treatment, or worse, another lecture.

But to her surprise, Susan walked into the house and found no tension at all. In fact, her father greeted her with a smile.

"How'd you like to visit your brother next week?" he asked.

"Wow, that sounds great!" Susan exclaimed, a little stunned. "But what's the catch? I thought the teachers at Rathmore said we shouldn't see Brian."

"Well, your father and I had a talk with Dr. Rathmore today," Susan's mother explained, "and, among other things, we talked about how much you miss Brian. Anyway, right off the bat, he understood what you're going through, and he suggested that you pay Brian a visit!"

"This is wonderful!" Susan cried happily. "I was afraid you guys had stopped caring about Brian."

"You know, honey," her father said, taking her hand, "we really do love Brian and we miss him a lot. After all, we haven't seen him in almost five weeks. Anyway, maybe if you see— maybe if we *all* see that Brian's okay, we'll feel much better."

The following Thursday Susan and her parents made the three hour trip to Rathmore. Sitting in the backseat of their station wagon, Susan was elated. The day was warm, the scenery along the highway was beautiful, and she was finally going to see her brother. Her parents had even written an excuse for her to get out of school for the whole day!

Yes, as far as Susan was concerned, things couldn't be better. Both her parents were hardworking lawyers. And when they weren't at their jobs, they were making sure the house was in tip-top shape, running errands, going to charity functions, or attending community meetings. They never seemed to have time to do anything with their kids, but here they were— taking the whole day off to spend it with her and Brian!

It was a little after 10:00 A.M. when they pulled through Rathmore's tall front gates and were greeted by a drab complex of austere, monolithic buildings. Susan hadn't known what to expect, and at first the place actually sent a chill down her spine. She relaxed a bit, however, when they drove further into the campus. Although everything looked kind of boring and sterile to Susan, at least the grounds were pleasant and spacious, with lush green lawns and tall shade trees.

They stopped in front of the large marble administration building where they met Dr. Rathmore, who was going to give them a personally guided tour of the campus. A tall, striking figure, the institution's headmaster was a robust looking man with few wrinkles in his well-tanned face. His gray beard was neatly trimmed, and he was impeccably dressed in a fine dark suit that showed off his athletic physique. At first Susan felt a bit intimidated by his imposing figure, but was soon put at ease by his gentle, soothing voice.

"Our program here at Rathmore is the most unique in the country," Dr. Rathmore said, as Susan and her parents followed him along a covered walkway from the administration building to the classrooms. "We offer a disciplined but nurturing environment. The rules, regulations, and expectations are clearly laid out for our youngsters, who not only have the benefit of learning from the finest teachers, but also have access to a complete medical staff, including psychiatrists."

"But my brother isn't nuts," Susan said, immediately regretting the remark.

"Dr. Rathmore wasn't implying that, dear," her mother said curtly. "You'll have to excuse our daughter, Dr. Rathmore. She's been very defensive about her brother lately."

Dr. Rathmore smiled. "That's quite all right, Mrs. O'Casey. Actually, I agree with Susan. Brian is *not* 'nuts,' as she so aptly put it. But like so many youngsters today he *is* floundering."

"What are you talking about?" Susan asked. She was hoping that Dr. Rathmore was going to say that Brian didn't belong at Rathmore.

"Your brother is looking for a sense of direction," Dr. Rathmore explained. "He needs appropriate guidelines for his behavior and only a school like Rathmore can provide them. You see, Susan, unfortunately, society in general, and our schools in particular, do not provide the proper guidelines that people like your brother need in today's world."

"I couldn't agree more," Susan's father said, nodding. "But it seems that there have been so many different programs aimed at badly behaved teens, and none of them have worked. What do you suppose makes Rathmore's program so effective? Why does it succeed where all the others have failed?"

"Oh, I wouldn't say they all failed—not completely, anyway." Dr. Rathmore flashed Mr. O'Casey a confident grin. "It's just that no other school has ever been able to claim the success rate that we can here at Rathmore."

Susan looked from her parents to Dr. Rathmore as they all laughed good-naturedly. What was that odd, knowing look the headmaster had just given to her parents?

"Brian is in his Social Interaction class right now," Dr. Rathmore said as he ushered them into a large white building. "Let's take a peek."

As they passed several classrooms, all of which had their doors wide open, Susan grew more and more uncomfortable with what she was seeing. All the kids sat in their seats like perfect little angels, their hands folded neatly on their desks and their eyes fixed straight ahead on the teacher.

Brian's Social Interaction class was no exception.

"And when we have a disagreement with our parents," the teacher was saying, "how do we conduct ourselves?"

Every hand in the room shot up. The teacher acknowledged one dark-haired girl, who immediately sprang to her feet.

"Because our parents are older and wiser," the girl stated like a programmed robot, "we should assume their opinion is the correct one."

As the girl sat down, a boy sprang up. For a moment, Susan didn't recognize him. Instead of the faded jeans and T-shirt he practically never took off, Brian now wore perfectly pressed slacks and a starched button-down shirt. And where was his beautiful long hair? Brian would never be caught dead with such a geeky-looking buzz cut. But, incredibly, the boy standing there ramrod straight, hands clasped behind his back like a toy soldier, was Brian.

"And if one continues to disagree with his parents, even after hearing them out," Brian stated, his voice a monotone, "one is wrong. A child should never insist when a parent says no. All this does is create dissension in the home."

"And if a child creates problems in the home, what are the consequences?" the teacher asked, raising an eyebrow.

"The consequences are . . . *painful*," answered Brian, smiling stiffly.

"Excellent, Brian," said the teacher. "You may sit down."

"Thank you," Brian said, taking his seat and neatly folding his hands on his desk.

Susan was dumbstruck. *That's not my brother*, she told herself. *That's some sort of computerized teacher's pet*. And then suddenly Susan smiled. *Oh, I get it!* she thought. *This is all a big act! Brian saw that I was here and he's just putting me on!*

But for the remainder of the class Brian never cracked a smile, and Susan was beginning to feel very uneasy by the time they left the classroom.

"That's remarkable!" her father exclaimed once they were out of the building. "I'm very impressed."

"I am, too," her mother agreed, although her voice was slightly tentative. Then she laughed nervously. "Actually, Brian seems, well, too good to be true."

Dr. Rathmore laughed along with her for a brief moment, then abruptly stopped. "Brian is new to the program," he said curtly. "And like many of our new students, he's probably trying a little too hard to please, a little too hard to fit in." He flashed a quick, tight smile. "But give him time, Mr. and Mrs. O'Casey. Little by little, your son will become more relaxed with his new view of the world."

New view of the world? Susan thought, a shudder moving down her spine.

After his Social Interaction class, Brian joined Susan and her parents for lunch outside the cafeteria. They sat at one of dozens of picnic tables set out on a large crescent of lawn behind the administration building.

"It's so nice to see you—Mom, Dad, Susan," he said stiffly. "I'm overjoyed you're here."

What a geek! Susan thought as she carefully studied her brother, still hoping that this was all some kind of an act.

"You look a little pale, Brian," her mother said. "Are you sure you're feeling all right, sweetheart?"

Brian gave his parents a big, generous smile. "I feel great!" he said enthusiastically. "In fact, I've never felt better!"

Susan grimaced and looked away. She couldn't bear seeing her brother like this.

"And how's the food, son?" Susan's dad asked, patting Brian on the shoulder.

"They have wonderful cafeteria food!" Brian said eagerly, like a household pet trying to please. "And lots of it! Boy, you can really chow down here!"

Wonderful cafeteria food? Susan thought. *He's putting us on!*

"What about the sports program, Brian?" her dad asked. "Are you getting outdoors a lot?"

"They have a fine sports program, Dad," Brian replied, sounding like a salesman. "However, Rathmore doesn't believe in contact sports, like football and soccer. They don't want any of the students getting hurt. We do have Ping-Pong and golf here," Brian added, "and I'm very fond of the nature walks."

The "very-fond-of-nature-walks" comment did it. Now Susan was convinced Brian was merely putting them on. But why hadn't he let her in on the joke yet?

"Someday, Dad," Brian went on, "maybe we could hit the old putting green together! Wouldn't that be fun?"

"Sounds good, Brian," Susan's dad said, now sounding a bit unsure himself.

"Hey, Brian, how's the music program here?" Susan asked, giving her brother a little wink. "I bet you can't wait to get home to listen to your own stuff."

"Actually, Susan, Rathmore offers any type of music we'd like to listen to," Brian answered pleasantly. "But I'm starting to get a taste for the old-time favorites, you know, like swing, light classical, old ballads—you know, the kind of music Mom and Dad like."

Susan had to put her hand to her mouth to keep from laughing. What a snow job Brian was pulling! He was totally making fun of the school without saying anything negative!

But Susan's mother was looking very puzzled. She looked deep into Brian's eyes and asked, "Are you saying that you don't like rock and roll anymore?"

"Rock and roll is not for me, Mom. Now I like the old fogey stuff—" Brian's hand shot to his forehead. "Ohhh," he groaned. "I didn't mean to say that. How could I possibly think of your music as old fogey stuff? That was a terrible thing for me to say!"

Susan snickered.

"Susan, don't you humor your brother," her dad snapped. "It's clear he's been making fun of us the whole time."

"No!" Brian cried, grimacing as though in pain, while at the same time trying to smile. "Gee, I'd never make fun of my fine, upstanding parents!"

"And you're still doing it!" Susan's mother cried.

"Well, I can see you still need to spend a great deal more time here at Rathmore!" her father said.

"Leave him alone!" Susan shouted, scowling at her parents.

"And as for you, young lady," her dad said, turning on her, "I will not tolerate any more of your rudeness—"

"Ooow!" Brian howled, no longer even making an effort to hide the pain. "My head! It—"

"Is there a problem here?"

Susan turned to see Dr. Rathmore coming over to where they sat at the picnic table.

"No problem," her father said, quickly collecting himself, seeming a bit intimidated by the stern-looking headmaster. "But I'm afraid Brian still needs a little work on his manners."

"I'm sorry to hear that," Dr. Rathmore said, throwing a glance at Brian. "I'm sure Brian is, too."

"For a minute you had me fooled," Susan's father said, looking directly at his son. "I thought you were sincere in what you were saying, and actually beginning to shape up. But I—"

"Dad, I really am trying," Brian said, a pained expression on his face.

"You don't feel well, do you, Brian?" Dr. Rathmore asked, stepping up and putting his hand on Brian's forehead.

Brian looked down at the table, seeming fearful of making eye contact with the headmaster. "You're right, sir," he said flatly. "I don't feel well."

"Susan," Dr. Rathmore said, looking her in the eye. "Would you take your brother to the infirmary? I'd like to speak to your parents alone."

"You were *soooo* funny," Susan said as she and Brian left the picnic table area and made their way toward the administration building. "Let's see, how did you put it?" She chuckled as the whole scene came back to her. "'Maybe the two of us could hit the old putting green together.' That was priceless!"

"Susan, I didn't—" Brian began.

"Sure you didn't!" Susan interrupted. "You're good, Brian. But you didn't fool me!" She laughed out loud and slapped her brother on the back just as they walked into the infirmary.

"Please conduct yourself properly," a middle-aged nurse dressed in white snapped at Susan. "That is no way for a young lady to act."

"Sorry," Susan said, trying not to smirk.

"How can I help you?" the nurse asked, fixing both her and Brian with a cold glare.

"I have a terrible headache, nurse," Brian said. "At first it felt like someone was reaching inside my brain and squeezing it. Now it feels like my brain's turning to liquid."

Susan couldn't contain herself and let out a howl of laughter. It wasn't *just* what Brian had said, it was *how* he had said it. Susan couldn't believe his self control. Brian had looked the woman dead in the eyes, and hadn't even cracked a smile!

The nurse stormed from the office.

"Look what you've done!" Brian cried. "The nurse is very mad." He gave Susan a hug, trembling all over. "I'm scared, Susan. What are we going to do?"

Susan burst into another fit of the giggles, laughing so hard she cried. "Stop it, Brian. You're gonna kill me!" she said, pulling out of his grip and grabbing a tissue from a box on the nurse's desk to wipe her eyes. It was then that she looked out the window and saw the nurse striding across the grounds to where her parents and Dr. Rathmore were talking in the lunch area. "Hey, get a load of this, Brian," she muttered. "Old nursie is going to tattle on us."

Brian, still trembling, came over to the window and watched his parents having an animated discussion with the nurse and Dr. Rathmore. Then, as the foursome headed away from the lunch area and began walking briskly toward the infirmary, he whispered in Susan's ear, "*Run!*"

"Huh?" Susan grunted. She was just about to ask Brian what he meant when her father entered the infirmary with her mother, the nurse, and Dr. Rathmore right behind him.

"Susan," her father said with a phony smile, "your mother and I have decided to enroll you here at Rathmore."

For a moment Susan couldn't believe what he was saying. Then she looked her father in the eye and suddenly knew the truth. "This wasn't a visit at all," she accused. "You were planning on leaving me here all along!"

"It's for your own good," her mother said quietly.

"Well, I hate to disappoint you guys," Susan said angrily, "but I'd rather be at this horrible place with Brian than anywhere with parents like you!" She grinned at Brian. "We'll have a blast, won't we, Brian?" she said, turning to her brother who wore a blank expression.

"We'll have to be on our very best behavior," Brian said flatly. "The code of conduct here is very strict. We learn to do as we're told at Rathmore. We learn that good conduct is essential to creating a harmonious environment for everyone."

Susan cocked her head and wrinkled her brow. What if her brother wasn't putting her on? What if he was being serious instead of sarcastic? A chill went down Susan's spine. Was it possible Brian had meant what he was saying?

"Mommm! I want to go home! Mom, Dad, are you there?"

A nurse, all in white, stood against a white wall. Her white canvas shoes squeaked on a white floor. She pulled a black window closed against a black night.

"Where am I?" Susan asked.

Nobody answered.

Fleetingly, Susan remembered her parents driving away from the school, and then the burning sensation in her head. After that there was nothing—until now. It was strange how little she remembered.

"Nurse?" Susan called.

But instead of the nurse, Dr. Rathmore's voice came from the end of her bed. "Yes?" he asked.

Though his tone was pleasant, the doctor had startled Susan. How long had he been there? she wondered. She tried to sit up, but her flesh seemed glued to the mattress. Struggling, she did manage to rise a little, but as she did, a huge patch of her back ripped off.

"My skin's coming off!" she screamed.

"That's just your imagination," Dr. Rathmore said calmly.

Susan reached to grab a clump of skin to prove it to the doctor but found herself gripping nothing but a white sheet.

Confused, she fell back on the bed, just as a nurse stepped up and pointed a flashlight beam into her eyes. "You're doing beautifully, dear" she said. "Now just relax, and everything's going to be fine."

"Wh-what's happened to me?" Susan stammered.

"You've had your first implant," Dr. Rathmore said coldly.

"My first *what*?" Susan cried.

"The first one is always hardest," the nurse said pleasantly.

"What are you talking about?" Susan demanded. "What will this implant do?"

"It will make you better," the nurse replied.

"Am I sick?" Susan asked, now more worried than ever.

"In a way," the nurse answered. "It's just that you don't know how to behave. But don't worry, dear. You will."

"I—I want to go home," Susan stammered.

"You can't," Dr. Rathmore said. "Not for a long time."

"You can't make me stay here!" Susan screeched. "You can't—" But suddenly a blinding pain shot through her head and she burst into tears.

The nurse looked sorrowfully at Susan, then clucked her tongue. "See how it hurts when you say the wrong thing?"

"Make it stop!" Susan screamed. It felt like nails were being pounded into her head.

"Will you be good?" Dr. Rathmore asked.

"Yes!" Susan screamed. "I'll do anything! I promise!"

Dr. Rathmore nodded to the nurse and suddenly the pain ebbed, then disappeared.

"See how easy it is?" the nurse said, "and how much better you feel when you're good?"

"Yes," Susan replied, blissful with relief from the pain sweeping through every fiber of her being.

"Now, I trust you'll be very careful in what you say and do?" asked the nurse.

"Oh, yes," Susan said enthusiastically. "I will be very careful. I promise."

Twelve long weeks passed before Kevin and Ellen O'Casey made their next visit to the school. They met with Susan and Brian in Dr. Rathmore's large, richly furnished office. At first the tension in the room was extremely thick, but within minutes the headmaster's calm demeanor gradually dispelled Mr. and Mrs. O'Casey's concerns. Besides, they could clearly see the obvious change for the better in Brian and Susan's behavior. Their children had glowing reports about the school, their outlook on life appeared to be totally positive, and they were more polite and respectful than they'd ever been before.

"I just hope you're being sincere now," Mr. O'Casey said to Brian, recalling his son's veiled sarcasm on their last visit.

"Oh, he's being sincere, Dad," Susan said, quickly jumping in to answer for her brother. "He was sincere before."

"Susan is right," Brian said. "And I apologize if anything I said before offended you. It really wasn't intentional, Dad."

"Well," said their mother. "I'm very pleased with what I'm hearing and seeing."

Dr. Rathmore smiled. "Brian, Susan," he said, "would you mind stepping out of the office for a moment? I'd like a word alone with your parents."

"Certainly," Brian and Susan said in unison. Then, like little robots, they walked out of the office and closed the door behind them.

"What would you like to speak to us about?" asked Ellen O'Casey as the door shut softly behind her children.

"Obviously the doctor wants to consult with us about Brian and Susan," Kevin said.

"No, not really," said Dr. Rathmore, placing his strong hands on his highly polished desktop. "I'm afraid it's a financial matter. Due to increasing costs we're needing to raise the tuition here at Rathmore." He cleared his throat. "It's a substantial, but necessary hike—from $19,000 to $25,000 a year per student—but I know you'll agree Rathmore is worth it."

Kevin O'Casey blinked. "B-but that's $50,000!" he gasped, his face flushing bright red.

"I'm truly sorry for this—" Dr. Rathmore searched for the right word. "—for this *inconvenience*, Mr. and Mrs. O'Casey."

"But we're already stretched to the breaking point," said Kevin O'Casey. "We just can't afford this!" He groaned and put a hand to his furrowing brow.

Ellen O'Casey heaved a sigh. "Well, Kevin," she said, "we're just going to have to tighten our belts a little more, even sell the house if we have to. For the children's sake—for *everyone's*—we simply must keep them at Rathmore."

Kevin O'Casey put his head in his hands. "I guess you're right," he finally said. "In the long run, I guess it's worth it."

Dr. Rathmore smiled sympathetically. "Believe me, I *do* understand how hard things can be these days. But," he said with a shrug, "we all have to do what we have to do." He rose from behind his impressive mahogany desk and led the way to the door.

"Thank you for your time," Ellen O'Casey said.

But all Kevin O'Casey could muster was a nod.

"I'll be looking forward to our next visit," Dr. Rathmore said, shaking hands warmly with them both. Then he gave a cursory wave of dismissal to Brian and Susan, who were sitting quietly in the waiting room, walked back inside his office, and shut his door.

Now alone, Dr. Rathmore walked across the deep pile carpet to the floor-to-ceiling bookshelf. There, he plucked a yearbook from its place. It was from the first year that Rathmore was in operation. With amused interest, Dr. Rathmore flipped to the graduation pictures of two of his first—and most successful—students. Two students who had known him as a younger man, but who now no longer remembered him—or even remembered attending the school, the implants in their heads making any such recollection impossible. But he remembered them—Kevin O'Casey and Ellen Cole, class of '65. Chuckling to himself, he remembered how they'd met and fallen in love here at school. "Ah, the perfect couple," Dr. Rathmore muttered to himself. "Perfect little sweethearts!"

He closed the book with a satisfied smile, returned it to the handsome walnut bookcase, then made his way to his sumptuous desk. Sitting in his high-back chair, he swiveled toward the window and glanced down at his glistening limousine in its private parking spot. He chuckled to himself, mentally comparing his own beautiful car to the stodgy old station wagon the impoverished, well-programmed O'Caseys drove. Swiveling back to his desk, he opened a ledger and turned his attention to preparing the O'Casey's new billing statement.

INNER EYES

Nema Stroud scowled at her guidance counselor, Ms. Goldblum, who was flipping through the pages of the New York Directory of Secondary Apprenticeship Programs.

"Nema," Ms. Goldblum said wearily, "you are fifteen. You've got to enroll in the advanced education track here at school or in one of the apprenticeship programs."

"I told you I'm outta here," Nema said. "No more school for me. I mean it."

Ms. Goldblum sighed. "All right. If school is out, you have to choose an apprenticeship program. I've already been through every offering in the directory from A to Z, and you have yet to express an interest in anything."

The dark-haired teenager sitting slouched beside the counselor's desk shrugged. "Well, go through it again."
Frowning at the girl's rudeness, Ms. Goldblum turned back to the first page. "Assistant air-tour guide. That might be fun," she said brightly.

"I don't think so," Nema said in a bored voice. "Go on."

Ms. Goldblum grimaced, then continued reading: "Bionics Assembler trainee . . . Cook's helper . . . Coroner's assistant trainee . . . Cybernetician's assistant—"

Nema cut the woman off. "Coroner's assistant. I like that."

Ms. Goldblum shrugged. Eager to be rid of the girl, she brought the computer on-line to current openings in the area and began filling out the student employee enrollment form. "You'll be reporting to International Medical Center, Monday at 8:00 A.M. sharp," Ms. Goldblum said. "Hmm," she mused, studying the monitor. "You're lucky. You're going to be working for Dr. Raymond Huntington. He's the inventor of Ocular Autopsy. In fact, in 2071, he won the Nobel Prize in Science for his experimental work in—"

"We can skip the history lesson," Nema said sarcastically.

Livid, Ms. Goldblum handed the form to the ill-mannered girl. "Fine, then. Remember, 8:00 A.M.—on the nose!"

At half past eight on Monday morning, Nema exited the underground moving walkway at the Park Avenue Corridor. Formerly a street, the Park Avenue Corridor was now a covered hallway inside the International Arts and Sciences Complex, which included the hospital where she'd be working.

"Where's room B73?" she asked an elderly man in the lobby.

"Oh, the coroner's office," he said pleasantly. "That's one level down, then make a left."

Without a word of thanks, Nema made her way downstairs, found room B73, and entered without knocking.

"May I help you?" a white-smocked young woman asked, looking up from a stack of files.

Nema waggled her enrollment form in front of the woman. "I'm Dr. Huntington's new assistant coroner—Nema Stroud."

The young woman arched her eyebrow and frowned. "You mean the new assistant orderly trainee," she said.

"Whatever," Nema said, flopping down in a chair.

"By all means, have a seat," the woman said sarcastically. "I'm Dr. Karen Ayala, the Assistant Coroner, and you, Nema, are clearly here to apply for a position in our apprenticeship program. You are also late. You were supposed to be here at eight o'clock. It is now a quarter to nine."

"Sorry," Nema said, rolling her eyes.

Dr. Ayala cleared her throat. "Your application, by federal law, has already been automatically processed. You are accepted into the program on a one month probationary basis at a minimum wage of $11.00 per hour, but you may be dismissed at any time if your work proves to be unsatisfactory." She forced a smile. "And promptness is *very* important."

Nema nodded, already taking a dislike to the woman. The feeling seemed mutual.

"Dr. Raymond Huntington is Chief of Staff and he is also the Director of Pathology, which is the study of disease and its effects. He is also the head of Radiology and Internal Medicine, and here in the coroner's office, he directs our work in the use of NOA, which stands for Non-intrusive Ocular Autopsy."

"What's that?" Nema asked without much show of interest.

"During an autopsy, Dr. Huntington and I don't cut into a corpse to determine the cause of death. We examine the interior of the body *visually*, using Radiographic Spectacles."

"You mean you can look into a dead body?" Nema asked, interested in spite of herself.

"Of course," Dr. Ayala said with a tight smile. "You've never heard of Radiographic Spectacles? Not even at school?"

"Must've been absent that day," Nema replied casually.

Dr. Ayala frowned, took a deep breath, then continued. "As part of your training program here at International Medical, you will be expected to familiarize yourself with Dr. Huntington's research and techniques, which include the invention of RBS and NOA, although your primary—"

Nema interrupted with a look of disgust. "You and Dr. Huntington *both* look inside dead bodies?"

"Yes," said Dr. Ayala, annoyed.

"Can he see into *living* bodies, too?"

"Not yet," said the young doctor. She opened a desk drawer, took out a glossy booklet and handed it to Nema. "Everything is explained in this booklet. As part of your training you are required to read it from cover to cover. Among other things, it explains the great progress that has been made in this area of scientific research."

Nema grimaced. "That's great. I already have homework on the first day!"

"The booklet is only twenty pages," Dr. Ayala said. "I suggest you read it tonight."

"How come I have to know all this stuff?" complained Nema, crushing the booklet into her purse.

"You're required to be familiar with the techniques used in the hospital," Dr. Ayala replied, trying to be patient, "although most of your work here will be of a manual nature."

"Like what?" Nema asked, raising an eyebrow.

"Like cleaning the autopsy room, bringing the cadavers up from the refrigeration area, and so forth." Dr. Ayala glanced at the wall clock. "Now, if you'll excuse me," she said, getting up, "I'm already running late. Take your enrollment slip and report to the scrub room. It's just down the hall."

Nema yawned. "Yeah, sure."

With a sigh, Dr. Ayala made her way back to the file room, relieved to be getting away from the new trainee.

In the scrub room, the supervisor, a quiet middle-aged man, gave Nema a smock to put on and told her to wash her hands. "Scrub them well—between each finger," he said sternly. "Then dip both your hands in there." He pointed to a porcelain bowl containing a thick white fluid.

Nema did as she was told, and to her amazement, when she removed her hands from the thick liquid, she was automatically wearing gloves.

"Weird!" Nema exclaimed. "What is that stuff?"

"Liquid rubber," the supervisor replied nonchalantly. "It hardens upon contact with skin—in this case, your hands— thereby immediately forming perfectly fitted surgical gloves."

The supervisor, whose name was Lloyd, then took Nema on a quick walk-through of the Frigiderium, where the dead were housed in banks of glass cubicles. Next he gave her a tour of the autopsy room, a large white marble chamber containing four heavy glass tables. Above each table a large light hung from the ceiling. Two workers stood at the counter cleaning instruments, then laying them on the glass tables in a precise order.

"This is the chute," the supervisor said, leading Nema over to a large transparent tube.

Nema noticed a broad conveyor belt inside. "What's that for?" she asked.

Lloyd smiled, glad that Nema was interested enough to ask questions. "That belt brings the bodies up from the morgue." He looked at Nema to see if she had any reaction. "Then you and another assistant will remove them from the chute and—"

The supervisor didn't finish what he was saying, the two workers stopped what they were doing, and everyone looked up. From a side door, a very tall, broad-shouldered man had entered the autopsy room with Dr. Ayala close at his heels. Due to his height and his shaved head, the man might have seemed menacing if he hadn't smiled warmly at everyone.

"That's Dr. Huntington," the supervisor said.

"Good morning, everybody," the doctor said in a relaxed, easy-going manner. "Excuse us." Then he and Dr. Ayala made their way into a small adjacent room.

"What's in there?" Nema asked.

"That's where they keep the Radiographic Spectacles," Lloyd answered. "We call them 'deadeye specs' around here. Dr. Huntington and Dr. Ayala are doing research on Electrolytic Polymer Contact Lenses in that room."

"What are *they*?" Nema wanted to know, no longer attempting to hide her fascination.

"Basically," the supervisor explained, "they're contact lenses for examining living tissue."

"Wow," Nema muttered, watching the two doctors return to the autopsy room wearing binocular-like glasses attached to their heads by plastic straps.

At a console in the center of the room, they dipped their hands into the liquid latex and were instantly wearing gloves.

"Okay, let's get to work," said Dr. Huntington to his staff.

The supervisor pushed a wall button and a buzzer sounded. Then a blue light came on inside the chute. With a quiet hum the conveyor belt began to move. Another worker hurried over, and Nema, a little scared, watched as the first corpse came down the transparent tube.

"It's really freaky," Nema told her boyfriend Thad later that night. They were rocking along on the antiquated L-train from Old Town Brooklyn to their homes in the New Jersey tenements. "I mean, he just looks at the dead bodies—looks right *into* 'em—and says what they died of."

"Huntington's invention for looking inside corpses is real cool," Thad said, admiring the new snake's head tattoo on his left bicep. He'd gotten it earlier that night. "I can't believe you never heard of it until today."

Nema frowned, a little embarrassed. "I'm supposed to study up on it tonight" she said, fumbling around inside her oversized purse, finally producing the booklet Dr. Ayala had given her.

Thad took the booklet and flipped through the first few pages. "Cool," he muttered. "It says here how the thing works."

Nema shrugged. "You can have the booklet if you want, Thaddy. I'm not gonna read it, anyway. I mean, what if I decide to quit—then I would've wasted a whole night studying something I could care less about."

Suddenly the aero-static brakes of the lumbering L-train hissed, and the multiple rows of synthetic iron wheels squealed.

"Here's my stop, Thaddy," Nema said, pulling herself to her feet as the train slid to a halt and its accordion doors flapped open. "See ya tomorrow?"

"Yeah," Thad mumbled, already engrossed in the booklet and not bothering to look up as Nema stepped off the train.

Nema didn't see Thad for the next few days, but when she came home Friday after work he was waiting for her on the front stoop of her plastiform house. It was almost identical to the hundreds of others in the run-down neighborhood.

"What's up, Thaddy?" she asked, sitting next to him on the stoop. "You look all excited."

"I am. I've been talking to this old guy in the rail yard named Benny, and he knows all about Dr. Huntington."

"Like what?" Nema asked.

"Like all about his research into these new contact lenses for looking inside of people," Thad replied. "By wearing them, a doctor can diagnose what's wrong with people."

Nema's eyes were glazing over with boredom, but Thad went on anyway. "Benny also told me that he heard from some friends of his who work at International Hospital that some big companies are willing to pay Dr. Huntington some heavy-duty money for those lenses, but the stupid guy is just going to give the invention away for free!"

"Who's he gonna give it to?" Nema asked absently, taking out a bottle of fluorescent purple nail polish.

"To International Hospital," Thad replied. "He's gonna give the lenses to them as soon as they're perfected. Then International is gonna make them by the truckload and donate them to doctors in poor countries."

"Well, that doesn't make any sense," Nema said, holding up her hand and admiring the garish polish. "Why would Dr. Huntington just give away something so valuable. He could make tons of money. Heck, if I could get a hold of those lenses I wouldn't give them to anybody. I'd sell them for top dollar and get out of this lousy neighborhood!"

"That's just it!" Thad exclaimed with a crooked smile. "Now that you're working with Dr. Huntington, you *can* get a hold of those lenses!"

Nema's dull eyes lit up.

"Well, Nema?" Thad asked, studying her face. "Do you think you can do it?"

"Yeah, I know exactly where he keeps them!" Nema exclaimed. "They're in the room right next to where I work!"

The following Monday afternoon Dr. Huntington entered the research lab adjoining the autopsy room where Nema Stroud worked. Moments later, almost banging the doors off their hinges, he re-emerged, a frantic look on his face. "The locker has been broken into!" he cried. "The EPCLs have been stolen!"

A few hours later, behind a deserted building on Hudson Street, Thad Willis paced restlessly. He looked at his watch, then gazed up and down the dismal, trash-strewn street. It was almost five-thirty and getting dark. Nema was supposed to have met him at four o'clock with the EPCLs, and from there they would take the tunnel-bus to Boston and sell the experimental lenses to a medical supply company. He was worried that she'd been caught, and even more worried that she'd betrayed him.

Meanwhile, Nema Stroud was sitting in the back of an L-train on her way to Manhattan. Smiling smugly, she patted her pocket. It contained a scrap of paper that stupid Thad had given her with the name of a buyer for the EPCLs.

Looking around warily at the other passengers, Nema decided to have a look at her prize—the extraordinary contact lenses that would make her rich. Carefully, she fished the box containing the lenses from her purse, then, not bothering to read the warning label taped to the side, she opened it. There sat two EPCLs. They looked just like ordinary contact lenses, except slightly larger.

The minute she saw them, Nema was dying to try them on. For a moment she hesitated—were they safe? Finally, unable to stop herself, she mumbled, "Oh, why not?" Then, glancing around at the other passengers, most of whom were dozing or reading, she bent over and popped a contact lens into each of her eyes. Then Nema Stroud looked up.

"I don't know what happened, officer," said the gray-haired little man to the Transit Authority Policewoman. The two stood outside the L-train where it had stopped at the Madison Avenue overpass. "I've never seen anything like it."

"Just tell me what you remember," said the policewoman, holding up a voice-activated micro-recorder.

The man ran a hand through his thinning gray hair and looked around at the crowd gathered on the overpass. Some of the other passengers were also being questioned by the police, but most were milling around, or talking amongst themselves. "I don't really know where to start," he said.

"Did you notice anything unusual prior to the incident?" the officer asked.

"No, I really didn't notice the girl at all. I was on my way home, sort of daydreaming, I guess. All of a sudden this girl in the back of the train makes a funny noise, sort of like 'Oooooh.' She was staring at the back of the head of the man sitting in front of her, as though she was suddenly fascinated with him. Then she started looking all around at everybody. At first, like I said, she sounded like she was amazed at something, but then she started to get frightened and very upset."

"Go on, please," the policewoman said, as she continued to record the man's statement.

"Well," the man said, looking a little uncomfortable, "that's when she jumped up and started staggering around, yelling at the top of her lungs."

"Yelling what?" the officer probed.

"It was hard making out most of it," the man said, "but she screamed for help several times. I—I tried to help her," he stammered, clearly getting emotional, "but she knocked me down. At that point, I just wanted to get away from her."

"Then what?" the officer asked.

The man shook his head. "The poor girl—she stumbled down the aisle, screaming like she'd lost her mind. And even though she kept begging for help, when anybody got near her she went wild."

"Wild?"

"Yeah, slapping and scratching at anybody who got in her way—including the motorman, who finally hit the emergency brake." The man shuddered. "We were all pretty scared. She was running around like a lunatic, kicking at the doors and smashing windows with her fists. She cut herself up pretty badly." He stopped for a moment, sighed, then continued. "It was like she was superhuman. I mean, she literally crashed right through one of the train doors. And then—" The man grimaced and walked over to the guardrail.

The policewoman followed him. "And then . . . ?"

The man pointed down at the tiered tracks below. "She ran straight down those tracks . . . right into a westbound train. It was going real slow, but it still hit her hard enough to send her flying." He pointed down at a descending People-Mover. "She landed on the moving sidewalk over there, and it carried her down to the next level. That's all I know."

"Thanks for your help," the officer said.

The man furrowed his brow. "Wonder what got into her?"

"So far, we don't have a clue," the policewoman said, gazing over the rail with the man. Below, police were restraining a crowd of onlookers as paramedics loaded an unconscious Nema into an air ambulance.

On the fourth floor of International Hospital, Nema awoke slowly. She'd endured seven hours of surgery on her battered body, and now, after nearly three days in a coma, she was opening her eyes for the first time. Turning her head, she gazed with opaque eyes at two male nurses. Though human in form, each was a skeleton, covered with masses of pink fleshy stuff. To Nema they looked like monsters. From their beating hearts, veins and arteries snaked off like roots from a tree, each bright red, pulsing with blood.

"She's coming to," one monster said.

"Call Dr. Huntington," said the other nightmarish being.

Forcing herself to look down the length of her own body, Nema was horrified to see that she had become one of them. "Noooo!" she cried, tearing at her eyes.

"Get the restraints!" one of the creatures yelled.

"Get away from me!" Nema cried, staggering from the bed.

"Stop her!" a monster yelled.

"My gosh, look at her eyes!" shouted another.

The two cornered her as they loomed closer, one cooed, "Now just relax, honey. We won't hurt you."

Shrieking frantically, she managed to dodge past them and crawl out the open window onto the ledge.

"I've got her!" one of the monsters screamed.

Looking down at her bony ankle, Nema saw a hand of veins and bone tightly holding onto her. She kicked free, but in doing so she lost her balance, and suddenly she felt herself falling backward. Emitting one long scream, Nema Stroud plunged eight stories to the street below.

The following day, the corpse of Nema Stroud lay on a glass autopsy table. The cause of death was immediately apparent.

"Massive internal injuries," said Dr. Huntington.

"Death was instantaneous," Dr. Ayala commented.

"I understand why she stole the EPCLs," he said. "She was going to sell them to a private business. But I don't understand why she would even think of putting them on. Didn't she see the warning label on the box?"

"We have no way of knowing," said Dr. Ayala.

"You gave her the required reading?" Dr. Huntington asked.

Dr. Ayala nodded. "During our first meeting."

"Didn't she understand that the EPCLs were not ready for use? The pamphlet clearly describes the problem we've been having. It explains that the lenses are so much like living tissue that their positive ions might cause them to immediately bond with the corneas."

Dr. Ayala peered closely at the opaque eyes of Nema Stroud. "That appears to be exactly what happened," she said. "The contacts melded into the eye tissue itself."

Dr. Huntington sighed. "Knowing the danger, why in the world would anyone put them on?"

"I think the answer's obvious, doctor," Dr. Ayala said.

Dr. Huntington raised an eyebrow. "And what's that?"

"She didn't know the danger."

"What do you mean?"

"I'm afraid Miss Stroud didn't do her homework."

MEMORIES OF THE DEAD

Fifteen-year-old Ricky Jones couldn't believe what he saw. "Hey Wendy," he yelled. "Come take a look at this!"

Wendy, one year older than her brother, ventured into the jungle of computer hardware that was his bedroom.

"What's up, geek?" she asked, finding Ricky, as always, sitting in front of his wall-size computer monitor. His unit, called the Zodiac 7000, had the "brains" of six other computers that Ricky had networked into a single system.

"I was doing research for my history paper on early space programs," Ricky began, "and I was just bringing up my menu to access the data banks on the Souyez-Mercury space probe that took place back in 2009. Anyway, I hit the wrong function key or something, and all of a sudden I saw something really freaky."

"Freaky? In what way?" Wendy asked.

"As in murder," Ricky replied bluntly. "I mean, I saw a portion of a murder in progress!"

"No way!" Wendy scoffed.

"No kidding," Ricky insisted. "The whole thing lasted only about a second, but I'm sure it was a murder. The audio port picked up a man screaming and things crashing all over the place, and for an instant I saw somebody with a scalpel in his hands." Ricky shuddered. "It was like I was seeing the murderer through the eyes of the person being murdered!"

"Do you remember what keys you pressed just before all this happened?" Wendy asked, her interest piqued.

"No, but the back-up memory support system will have it," Ricky replied, his eyes magnified behind his thick glasses. "I'm accessing it right now."

Like a digital clock going at a thousand miles an hour, codes rolled in ever-changing sequences on the monitor. Then everything stopped abruptly and the audio port said in a robotic monotone, "*YOUR PREVIOUS COMMAND WAS F3, D5.*"

"Bingo!" Ricky cried, quickly punching in F3, D5.

Instantly, a murky image appeared on the screen, and over the audio port came the sounds of a gurgling scream and things falling and breaking. Next came the sound of laughing, followed by a voice yelling, "*MNR is my baby!*"

As the two kids remained fixated on the computer screen, an elderly balding man stumbled into view. He was clutching his face and neck, both dripping blood. Then he disappeared and the profile of a younger man with long hair appeared. His mouth was open in mid-scream, and he was holding something shiny in his hand. "*Doctor!*" the young man yelled, running toward the older man as something off-screen was knocked over with a loud bang. Then for an instant, a shadowy figure appeared in the background running up a set of stairs and turning to look back over his shoulder.

"Wow!" Wendy gasped. "This is unbelievable!"

She and Ricky continued to watch with open mouths as shadowy legs disappeared up the stairs and a full-face view of the long-haired young man reappeared, a greenish light glinting off the scalpel he held. *"Too far!"* screamed an off-screen voice as the scalpel tumbled from the youth's hand and he staggered away as if hurt. Then the screen went blank.

Ricky was about to comment when suddenly someone on the screen asked, *"Why?"* The question came out liquid-sounding, almost like a gurgle. Then the older man reappeared, his bloody face pressed against the monitor and his hand clawing the air. He was up so close to the screen that Ricky and Wendy actually recoiled. It was as though the man was trying to escape from where he was *through* the monitor screen.

"Save it!" Wendy yelled. "Hurry before it erases!"

Ricky's hands flew across the computer keys as though he were a demented pianist. "I think I've gotten it all!" he cried, letting out a sigh as he hit G8 BACKSAVE, pounding the key like it was the final note of his masterpiece.

For a moment the screen went blank, then new footage appeared of something that went on *before* the murder.

"It's the old guy who was murdered!" Wendy exclaimed.

And there, before them on the screen, was the elderly man who was later to be murdered. He was in a different room now, sitting at a desk scribbling notes on an electric slate while he stuffed a sandwich into his mouth. An attractive young woman walked past. *"Time for your ten o'clock class,"* she said, her voice coming through loud and clear from the Zodiac 7000 audio port. The man on the monitor swiveled around and was about to speak . . . when the monitor went blank.

"Darn!" Wendy cried. "I guess that's all we get to see."

"Well I've seen enough," Ricky said, a slight tremor in his voice. "What did I access?"

"Maybe it was a movie or something," Wendy suggested.

Ricky didn't even bother to comment. He punched the BACKPRINT key, and immediately a printout of what they had just seen spewed out of the computer's printer.

"Maybe we should call the cops," Wendy murmured, studying the black-and-white horror show they'd just captured on paper.

"I don't know," Ricky replied. "I mean, this could just be some computer hacker getting his kicks." He glanced at the printout. "I've got to study this before we—"

Suddenly their mom peered into the room. "Didn't you guys hear me calling you?" she asked. "Dinner's ready."

Ricky frowned, reluctant to leave the mystery unsolved. He was just about to say he wasn't hungry when his mother added, "Now remember, after dinner we're going over to the Corbins, and I expect you guys to be on your best behavior."

Ricky and Wendy exchanged knowing glances. With a mutual sigh they headed downstairs, ate dinner, and then spent a boring evening with Mr. and Mrs. Corbin and their three dweeby daughters.

It wasn't until after school the next afternoon that Wendy and Ricky began studying the murder mystery again. First they enlarged and enhanced several of the images. Then, after studying them all carefully, Wendy pointed out that the attractive female who appeared in a few frames was wearing a sweatshirt with the initials UCTSD across the front.

"UCTSD stands for University of Computer Techtronics at Santa Domingo," she commented.

"That's only a few miles from here!" Ricky exclaimed. "And I've heard they're doing all kinds of weird computer research. Come on, let's go check it out!"

"Wait!" she cried.

They gazed at the screen in disbelief. The same terrifying scene they had watched the day before was reappearing.

"Did you punch in the replay code?" Wendy asked.

"No. It's replaying all by itself!" Ricky gasped.

Wendy stared at the screen. "It's as though somebody else is replaying it and somehow the Zodiac 7000 is picking it up."

The instant the sequence came to an end, the monitor lit up with written text.

"Wow!" Ricky quickly hit the commands for save and print.

"Looks like some kind of an essay or something," Wendy said, reading the printout over Ricky's shoulder. "'MORDANT NEUROLOGICAL RECALL. DR. RANDALL LISTON.'"

"Who's Randall Liston?" Ricky wanted to know.

"The guy who wrote the paper, nerd," Wendy said matter-of-factly. "Shut up and let me read!"

Ricky read along silently as Wendy read on out loud: "'Cryonics was developed during the 20th century. It is based on the discovery that when a human body is frozen immediately after death it remains essentially unchanged for years. Since chemical activity in the cells comes almost to a stop, decomposition that normally takes place after death does not occur. This is true not only of the body but also of the brain.

Initial work in accessing the memories of the dead was begun by Dr. Miriam Handel in 1999. Doctor Handel—'"

"Accessing the memories of the dead!" Ricky exclaimed. "Is *that* what this is all about?"

"*Shuush!*" Wendy hissed, then went back to the printout: "'Dr. Handel referred to this technology as M.N.R.—Mordant Neurological Recall, and I, Dr. Randall Liston, have made much progress since Dr. Handel's early experiments in the field. Now I have the capability of eliciting complete audio-visual playbacks of the deceased's last memory. The process is simpler than I had ever imagined since the dentate fissures in the brain are so similar to the memory chips in a computer. In fact, all that's needed is to locate the desired 'chip' and tap into it with electrodes. To date, I have successfully accessed the memories of a chimpanzee and a rat. Obviously, the next step is to access and play back the memory of a human.'"

"Well, I think we now know what accidentally came up on my computer!" Ricky said excitedly.

Wendy nodded. "Yup. I think Dr. Liston, who perfected Dr. Handel's Mordant Neurological Recall and then wrote this essay, was murdered—and *we* saw it in his memory bank!"

"And," Ricky said, "we also saw the murderer—the long-haired guy with the scalpel!"

Wendy sat down, her brow wrinkling in thought. "Hmm, the way I figure it, the long-haired guy wanted to get his hands on the discovery of this M.N.R. thing."

"And then the murderer froze the corpse cryogenically," Ricky said, his eyes huge, "put electrodes on the head of the corpse, and accessed his victim's memory of his own murder!"

"And we saw the playback," Wendy said.

"Yup," Ricky replied, "and I've got an idea how we can see even more." He quickly made his way from the Zodiac 7000 to a small, obsolete-looking computer in a corner of his room. "Let's boot up the Ibex 51."

"Why mess with that old thing?" Wendy asked.

"Simple," Ricky replied. "We'll access the files of the *Daily Herald* and find out if anyone reported Dr. Randall Liston's murder. Then we'll see if there was any foul play reported at the University of Computer Techtronics at Santa Domingo."

After hours of searching through almost a year's worth of newspapers, magazines, and files, they were just about to give up. Then suddenly, there it was—a small article in *Comp-Tech* magazine from only eight days before!

"That's him!" Wendy exclaimed.

On the monitor in front of them was a picture of Dr. Randall Liston. According to the article, dated July 29, 2018, Liston was a professor of computer sciences at UCTSD, and he was being given an award for his "research linking computer and medical technology." The article went on to explain that Liston would soon be unveiling a startling new discovery.

Ricky gasped. "Look who's behind Liston!"

"The long-haired guy," Wendy said, dumbfounded.

Ricky grinned. "Now, with just a little more evidence, we can call the police."

A half-hour later, Wendy and Ricky found themselves standing in front of the wall directory of UCTSD's Computer Sciences building. Dr. Liston's office was on the first floor, room 114.

Racing down the hall to Liston's office, they were not prepared for the surprise they walked into when they entered the room.

There, working at a desk in the reception area, was the attractive young woman they had seen on the computer monitor who'd said something to Dr. Liston about his ten o'clock class. On her desk was a nameplate: BRENDA TORRES.

"May I help you?" she asked.

"We'd like to talk to Dr. Liston," Ricky said.

"I'm sorry," the young woman replied, "but Dr. Liston is out of town."

"Where did he go?" Wendy asked, looking around as if she might spot his corpse under a desk. Then her eyes fell on a closed door with the word "LAB" on it. "Uh, Dr. Liston didn't mention he was going anywhere to us," Wendy said evenly as she looked into the woman's eyes. "And it's very important we—"

"It was a last-minute trip," the young woman blurted out. "May I ask who you are?"

"Who are all these people?" Wendy countered, pointing to a group photo on a bulletin board behind the woman. In the photo were Dr. Liston, Brenda Torres, and the long-haired killer. The young woman looked at the picture, then turned back to Wendy, a puzzled looked on her face. "That's me, Dr. Liston, and Norman Eno, Dr. Liston's research assistant."

"Could we talk to Norman?" Ricky asked.

"No," the woman said, her voice growing edgy. "Norman's busy in the basement lab, and he left word that he's not to be disturbed. Now, may I ask what you want? I'm very busy and—"

"Any messages for me, Brenda?" a preppy-looking man interrupted, plunking himself down at the desk next to Brenda's.

"No, no messages, Tom," Brenda Torres said.

He turned to Ricky and Brenda. "And who might you be?"

"We might be leaving," Wendy said as she and her brother made a quick exit.

Outside the Computer Sciences building they found a bench where they could talk in private. "Something's going on!" Wendy said excitedly.

"I'll bet you anything that Eno is in the basement lab with Liston's frozen corpse," Ricky declared. "And he's probably plugging into the old guy's brain as we speak. We've got to get down to that lab!"

"Oh no we don't!" Wendy cried. "What we do now is call the police!"

"But we still don't have proof that Liston's actually dead," Ricky protested.

"We've got proof enough!" Wendy argued.

"We haven't got anything yet," Ricky said, getting up from the bench. "All we've got are pictures that came through a computer and a bunch of theories! I'm going back there to see if I can find a way to get into the lab."

"Well, *I'm* calling the cops," Wendy said, stomping off. "And if you had any brains you wouldn't go near that place."

Ignoring her, Ricky headed back toward the Computer Sciences building. In the corridor he passed Brenda Torres. She gave him a look of disapproval but kept walking.

Perfect, Ricky thought. *Maybe I can get some information from that guy who came into Liston's office while we were talking to Brenda Torres.* Hurrying along to room 114, he opened the door and found the preppy-looking guy smiling at him.

"Oh, you're back," the young man said. "May I help you?"

"I, um, loaned Norman a book on networking yesterday, and I need it back because—"

"He's down in the lab," the young man interrupted. "You can go talk to him if you want, but don't be surprised if he bites your head off. Norman's been acting weird lately. If I go anywhere near him he yells at me to go away."

"Are you a friend of his?" Ricky asked.

"Sort of," the young man replied, extending his hand. "I work for him and Dr. Liston. I'm Tom Tarter. And you are—?"

"Ricky Jones," Ricky replied, shaking the man's hand.

"Well, Ricky. Let's see if Norman left your book up here," Tom said, glancing around the office. "What was the title?"

"*Networking Zodiac*," Ricky said, pretending to look around for the non-existent book.

"Hmm, it doesn't seem to be here," Tom said. "Oh well, what the heck." With a laugh he headed for the lab door, pulling keys from his jacket pocket. "Maybe we can intrude on grouchy Norman long enough to get your book back."

With that, Tom opened the door and peered into the semi-darkness below. "Hey, Norm!" he called. "Somebody named Ricky is here to see you!"

Nervously, Ricky followed Tom down the first few steps. Behind him, the self-closing door hissed shut.

"Sorry to bother you, Norman," Tom said, but his words were drowned out by several voices coming from a computer audio port. "Hey, Norm?" Tom persisted. "Are you down here?"

Getting no answer, Tom continued to descend into the room filled with a maze of computers. Across the room, almost hidden by hardware and oversized monitors, Ricky could see a familiar figure—the long-haired man. He seemed completely engrossed in what he was doing and unaware of Ricky and Tom making their way toward him.

"Hey, Norm," Tom called. "Come up for air for a second! We just want to get Ricky's book and—" Suddenly Tom stopped, then recoiled in horror. Strapped to a chair, the frozen corpse of Dr. Liston stared back at him.

"Dr. Liston!" Tom gasped, staring at the dead man. "Norman, what is this? What have you done!"

Feeling sick to his stomach, Ricky stared at the corpse of Dr. Randall Liston. Cables ran from a computer to holes that had been driven into the man's head, and grisly images—Dr. Liston's memories—played on the monitor like a bizarre movie.

Despite Tom's exclamation of horror, Norman remained completely absorbed in what he was doing. Spectral, colored lights from the monitor played on his wide-eyed face, alternately dimming and brightening in a dozen ghostly hues. Then Ricky saw the tube in *Norman's* wrist, the holes in *Norman's* skull, and the wires and computer feeds sprouting out of *him* just like they sprouted out of Dr. Liston.

"Well now," Tom said, turning to Ricky, his voice dripping with sarcasm, "do tell me how you lent a book to Norman yesterday when Norman was *dead* yesterday."

Ricky looked with terror-filled eyes back and forth from the figure of Tom creeping toward him to the corpse of Norman. "Y-you killed them both!" he gasped. "But why?" Then Ricky dimly recalled something he'd seen on his monitor at home. It was a fleeting image of a *third* person—the one running up the stairs in the background.

"They were both dead yesterday," Tom said with a touch of glee. "M.N.R. was *my* project. They stole my work and claimed it as their own." Then, Tom pulled a familiar object from his pocket—a scalpel. "At least I found a way to fit them into my research!" He laughed maniacally. "They'd be pleased, don't you think?"

In abject terror, Ricky backed away as Tom's hand suddenly shot out and grabbed him by the collar. "And you get to be a part of it, too!" Tom said, as he raised his weapon and . . .

"Police! Drop it!" someone yelled from the top of the stairs.

"Ricky!" screamed a familiar voice. "Are you all right?"

The scalpel clattered to the floor as Tom's hands went up and Ricky scrambled to safety.

Wendy and the police officer clattered down the metal steps, followed by a campus security officer who grabbed Tom's arms and cuffed them behind his back.

"I don't understand," Wendy said, pulling away from the bear hug she was giving Ricky. "I thought the long-haired man was the killer."

"No," Ricky replied. "We misunderstood what we saw on the monitor. Tom Tarter was the murderer. He killed them both, Dr. Liston *and* Norman Eno." Ricky walked woodenly to the icy corpse of Liston then to that of Eno, both sitting frozen and rigid in chairs. The monitor in front of Eno had captured Tom Tarter's face, filled with murderous rage.

"Why did he do it?" Wendy asked.

Ricky was a long time answering. "I don't know all the details." He looked from one corpse to the other. "But *they* do. They remember it all, and everything needed to convict Tom Tarter is stored in their heads."

"So," Wendy said with a grin. "I guess you could say that the murderer will be convicted by his own spoils!"

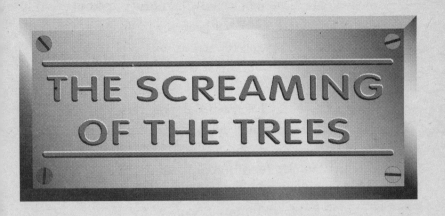

THE SCREAMING OF THE TREES

'm sitting on my bed. Mom's coming down the hallway. *Drag . . . shuffle . . . bang. Drag . . . shuffle . . . bang.* She limps into view and stands there in the doorway. I don't like to look at her, with her bent leg and her distorted face. After the accident, the doctors tried to fix her face with plastic cheekbones and synthetic flesh, but she still doesn't look like the mother I remember.

"It's time for your appointment, Rebecca," she says.

I turn away from her. She reminds me of everything I want to forget. "I—I dreamed about Daddy again," I yell over the radio, which I keep on as loud as it will go. "He was in my room hacking away at trees like a crazy man. It—it was awful, just awful the way those trees bled and screamed out in pain."

"Tell the psychiatrist, honey," Mom says. "I can't hear it anymore. I can't hear any of it anymore."

"I'm tired of talking to doctors!" I yell at her. "I'm not going to see them anymore."

"Yes, you are," she replies, calm as always. "You'll see this one. He says he understands your problem."

"Will he be able to stop the screaming?" I challenge her.

Mom doesn't answer my question. "Just get ready, Rebecca," she says.

"What's the use?" I screech, getting very agitated. "I've seen a thousand doctors and not one of them has ever done a single bit of good!"

Mom just stands there looking tired and sad. She's not angry at Dad like I am. She doesn't blame him for my torture, her disfigurement . . . or Tommy's death.

"Well?" I demand. "Will going to this doctor change things. Will it bring Tommy back?"

She shakes her head and a tear rolls down her cheek. "No, Rebecca," she says. "It won't bring back Tommy or your father."

Seeing her tears my anger wilts immediately. "I'm sorry," I say, and pat the bed I'm sitting on. "Come and sit down, Mom."

She comes and sits next to me.

I take the reasonable approach. "Mom, I wouldn't mind going to see this new psychiatrist if it would make the screams go away. But it won't, and we both know that, don't we?" I smile at her. "Wouldn't you agree that seeing another psychiatrist is kind of silly? I mean, I'm not crazy, am I, Mom?"

She looks at me with her one good eye. The one destroyed in the accident looks like a squashed blue grape. She puts her arm around me. "No, honey," she says. "You're not crazy. I just want you to be happy again, to grow up and—"

She stops herself when she sees how I react to the word *grow*. "Please, Rebecca," she says. "Try this one last doctor. He says he understands."

"It won't do any good," I say loudly, shouting over the blaring radio and the screams inside my head. "But I'll go. Even if it's just a waste of time."

It's a three-minute drive to the doctor's office. By solar-car, nothing in Mortonville, Iowa, is more than a half-hour away, especially since there's hardly any traffic anymore. Mortonville is a dinky little town that sits on a bluff overlooking the prairie. There's a virtual reality theater, a few office buildings, and a hydroponics plant where almost everybody in town works. Those are the big buildings, the rest are just little stores and houses, most of them boarded up. A lot of people have already left Mortonville. The others will follow.

The new psychiatrist's office turns out to be the entire second floor of a wood-frame house. It's a very old building, probably built back in the twentieth century. Mom decides to wait in the car as I knew she would. She doesn't like people to see her face. Besides, she doesn't want to attempt climbing the stairs with her bad leg.

"I'll be right back!" I call to her, then I run up the stairs and bang on the door. When nobody answers, I open the door and walk into the empty waiting room. "Anybody here?" I yell.

When I don't get an answer, I sit down and look for an old magazine to read. There are always old magazines in waiting rooms, but not in this one. In fact, there's nothing in here but a bunch of chairs lined up against the wall. Music comes from somewhere, and I close my eyes and try to listen over the noise in my head.

"Rebecca Gatkin?" someone calls out.

I look up and see this big, stoop-shouldered man looking at me. He's wearing blue jeans, a sports jacket, and sandals. His hair is shaggy and down to his shoulders.

"I'm Jim Babbitt," he mumbles, then wanders back toward wherever he came from. "Follow me," he says over his shoulder, sort of like it's an afterthought.

The guy's weird, but I follow him down a hallway and into another room. Somber cyber-rock is playing. The room is big and messy, not at all like the offices of the other doctors I've seen.

"Sit wherever you'd like," he tells me.

"Please turn up the music," I say, ignoring his directive.

He turns up the music, then starts clearing a bunch of books and papers off his desk. He looks around for a place to put the stuff, then decides to just dump it on the floor. I circle the room to make sure all the windows are closed. For a minute I look out across the prairie to the highway in the distance. Beyond the highway is something I don't want to see.

"Sit wherever you'd like," Dr. Babbitt says again.

"This okay?" I ask, dropping down and sitting cross-legged on the floor.

He shrugs and starts to sit down in his desk chair, but there's a cat asleep on it. "This is Maggie," he says, gesturing toward the pure white cat with pinkish ears. He picks the animal up and takes it into his arms as he sits down. "Do you like cats, Rebecca?"

"Yes," I tell him. "I used to have one."

"And what happened to your cat?" the doctor asks.

"It went nuts, so we had to put it to sleep," I say matter-of-factly, like that happens to most household pets.

"That's a shame," Dr. Babbitt says, gently stroking his cat.

That's when I notice for the first time that Dr. Babbitt's eyes have deep circles under them and a kind of haunted, faraway look as well.

"Do you know who I am?" I ask real loud. I'm trying to shout over the noise in my head, but I also feel the need to get this guy's attention.

He nods.

"Then you know about my dad and what he did, right?"

"A little," he replies quietly.

"Do you want me to tell you about it?" I ask.

He lifts Maggie off his lap and drops her gently to the floor. "Sure," he says as the cat arches her back, yawns, then patters over to me. "But first, I need to ask you a question. Would that be all right with you, Rebecca?"

"Was that the question?" I ask snidely as Maggie eyes me up and down, then hops into my lap.

Dr. Babbitt raises an eyebrow and smiles, but otherwise does not acknowledge my little joke. "Tell me, Rebecca," he says, "Why do you shout so much?"

"It's just a habit," I yell at him.

He smiles. "Well, we'll talk about your 'habit,' but would you try to talk softer in the meantime? When you shout, it makes it hard for me to talk to you."

"But you won't be able to hear me!" I holler.

"I'll be able to hear you just fine. Just try me," he says, dragging a wooden chair close to where I'm sitting on the carpet. He plunks down on it, and leans forward over the backrest. "Tell me about yourself, Rebecca," he says, looking me straight in the eyes.

"What do you want to know?" I yell.

Wincing, he pats down the air in front of him, gesturing me to lower my voice.

I take a deep breath. "What do you want to know?" I ask again, this time in a normal voice.

"Whatever you want to tell me."

I shrug. "Well, I'm fifteen," I begin. "Until three years ago, I lived in Oregon. Then we started moving from place to place. After we left Oregon, we lived in about a zillion different cities and towns before we ended up in Mortonville."

"Why do you move so often?" he asks.

"I was going bonkers," I reply. "You see, everyday I'd wake up and see the forest. It made me sick inside . . . and scared."

"Scared of what?"

"Of the trees," I say, as if he should know that already. "Even dead, they still seem to have the power to kill." My voice is rising but I can't seem to stop it. "It's like they're angry or something! It's like they're angry at me, when it's my father who's to blame."

"Was your father *really* to blame?" Dr. Babbitt asks.

"Of course he was!" I scream. "Everybody knows that my father is responsible for *all* the deaths!"

Dr. Babbitt indicates that I should keep it down. "Who did your father kill?" he asks, knitting his brow. His eyebrows crawl toward each other like two furry caterpillars.

"I thought you said you know who I am," I say, sort of sarcastic. "If you know who I am—if you know the name Rebecca Gatkin—then you know the name *Robert* Gatkin. And that means you know he killed nineteen people—twenty, including himself!"

For almost a full minute Dr. Babbitt says nothing. In fact he looks kind of confused. Finally he says, "I—I guess I'm not up on all the details."

"Well, let me fill you in, Doctor," I say angrily. "One of the nineteen people my father killed was my little brother Tommy!"

"I'm sorry, Rebecca," Dr. Babbitt admits, sounding tired. "I guess I don't know as much about your father as I should. Tell me about him."

I see my dad in my head. I see his brown eyes, thin face, and long neck. He looks like a male version of me. I smile for a moment, remembering how he held his head forward. *Always sticking his neck out*, I think, grinning even more.

"Dad was very ambitious," I tell Dr. Babbitt, "and very smart. He was always in a hurry to accomplish whatever came next." I pause for a moment. "And it wasn't just money he was after. Oh, that was part of it, all right. But what Dad *really* wanted was success."

"Do you think he cared more about being a success than he did about you?"

"No doubt about it," I say, not even having to think over the question. "Success was more important to him than me, or my mom, or anything."

"Tell me about your mom . . . before the accident," Dr. Babbitt says, getting that faraway look in his eyes again. His head is kind of cocked, as though he's listening to something outside of the room.

"When I was little, she was fun and real sweet and sort of down-to-earth." I smile at the thought, but my smile vanishes the second her face—the way it looks now—pops into my head. "And she was real pretty . . . until Dad screwed things up. He got to be a hotshot scientist and he'd go around to different lumber companies and give them advice on ways to improve their yield so they could get richer. He got richer too, and we moved into a big house in the woods near Lake Everett."

In my mind I see the rosewood floors, the marble decking, and big windows overlooking the boats floating on beautiful blue-green water.

"And how did your father's success affect your mom?" Dr. Babbitt asks, bringing me back to his office.

"She changed completely," I say flatly.

"In what way?" he urges.

"She turned into a big socialite snob. We had two boats, an aqua-chopper, and a few hydro-cars to run around in. And all kinds of important people were always coming over to our house for big fancy parties."

"How about you?" Dr. Babbitt runs his hand through his long hair. "How did these things change you?"

I think for a minute. "Well, naturally, other kids were jealous of me and Tommy because we were so rich. And to be honest, I liked feeling superior to everybody else. Of course, this was before I found out what my dad's invention, Xylem 40, was really doing. It was before all the killing started." I feel myself starting to get excited. "Do you want me to tell you about it?"

"Yes, but stop yelling," Dr. Babbitt says. "Can you try to do that?"

I hadn't realized I had raised my voice again. "Okay," I say softly. "I'll try."

He nods.

"At first, Xylem 40 just did what it was supposed to, and they sprayed the stuff over a thousand acres around Lake Everett with these big aqua-planes. *Zoom! Zoooom! Zoooooom!* One after the other, the planes kept flying back and forth over the trees and coating them with Xylem 40."

Maggie the cat is still in my lap. She starts licking my hand. Her raspy tongue tickles. "Ever see an airplane bleed?" I yell at the doctor.

"No," he says again, gesturing for me to lower my voice.

"Well, that's what it looked like," I tell him. "Xylem 40 is red, and when the planes sprayed the stuff, it looked like blood was spewing out of them, not chemicals."

Dr. Babbitt rests his head on the chair-back and waits for me to go on.

"Do you know what Xylem 40 was supposed to do, Dr. Babbitt?" I ask.

"Not really," he replies.

"Well, normally, most trees grow to a maximum height of about three hundred feet. Xylem 40 was supposed to double that and cut the time in half that it takes a tree to mature. Anyway, the lumber companies were overjoyed."

Dr. Babbitt's eyes widen. "And your father invented Xylem 40 on his own?"

"Yeah, though a couple of other jerks helped." I make a face, and for a minute watch Maggie all curled up and content in my lap. "At first the stuff was a great success. Everybody was happy and getting richer than ever. That was the first year. But the next spring everybody realized that Xylem 40 had been carried in pollen to unsprayed trees, and those trees were growing twice as fast, too."

I look at Dr. Babbitt to see if he's still with me. He nods, and I go on.

"Anyway, they started growing faster and faster. Four hundred feet, five hundred, up to six hundred feet—that's how tall they were getting. It would have been great, except that the roots couldn't keep up with the growth of the trunks. And the trunks were getting weird inside—hollow, like pumpkins, all rotten and pulpy."

"It doesn't sound like they would make very good lumber," Dr. Babbitt comments.

"They were worthless as lumber, but still they kept growing faster and faster. I mean, you could actually *see* them growing, and you could *hear* them as they grew." I shudder, remembering the first time I heard them cry out, and then I look deep into Dr. Babbitt's eyes. "Have you ever heard a tree scream? It's a horrible screeching sound like a million fingernails on a million blackboards." I shudder again. "Anyway, then came the horrendous crashes as they started falling. You see, their roots couldn't support them, and they fell all over the place . . . sometimes on people. Mrs. Madison, one of my mom's best friends, was the first person killed."

"Is that how you lost your brother?" Dr. Babbit asks.

"He and my mom were crushed inside our car, trying to escape. That's how my mom got so hurt and disfigured . . . and how Tommy died."

"How were you able to escape harm?" Dr. Babbitt asks.

"My dad put me on one of the aqua-choppers airlifting people out. I begged him to come, too. I was screaming at him over all the noise. But he was like a zombie, standing there staring at what he'd done, watching the trees come down, one after the other, crunching people. That's when he just walked into the forest . . . and never came back."

Dr. Babbitt is quiet for a moment and so am I. Then he asks real softly, "And how's your mother now?"

"Mom was in a hospital in Copeland, Oregon for a long time, and they took me there to be with her. She finally got better—more or less—that winter. Winter is the non-growth season for trees. But then in the spring it started happening in the woods around Copeland, too. The trees were getting gigantic. You had to yell to be heard over the sounds of their growing pains. It was driving me crazy. We moved to Nebraska, out on the plains, as far away from forests as we could get. But in my head I still hear the trees. That's why I started yelling, see? To be heard over their screams."

Dr. Babbitt nods and smiles warmly. "A lot of people have developed a habit of yelling like you have, Rebecca. They come to me because I understand."

"Really?" I ask. "You've seen other patients like me?"

"Quite a few, but none as closely connected to the disaster as you are."

"Were you able to cure them?" I ask eagerly.

"Yes, though it was easier with those who got out early, like me."

"Like *you*?" I can't believe what I'm hearing.

Dr. Babbitt smiles warmly. "I had a yelling habit too, Rebecca. I was living in Eugene, Oregon back in 2032, when it all started. I couldn't take it, so I moved here to Mortonville."

"So you know how hard it is to get the sound out of your head?" I ask, feeling an immediate sense of kinship.

"Yes," he says, a sad look on his face.

"But if it's just the memory of the sound, you can keep it out then, right?" I ask.

"Mnemonic auditory hallucination is the fancy term for what you're talking about," Dr. Babbitt says. "And the answer is yes, but it's not easy."

I nod. "Yeah, the hard part," I say, forcing myself not to yell, "is trying to separate the memory of the sound from the real sound of new trees growing."

He nods in understanding. "I suppose that's why your cat had to be put to sleep. Animals hear sounds more acutely than humans do."

I nod, then look down at the doctor's cat still sound asleep in my lap. "Did you have Maggie when you lived in Oregon?" I ask, petting the cat's soft fur.

"Yes, Rebecca."

"Well, how come she didn't go crazy?"

"I had her eardrums removed." He paused. "That's one method I suggest to patients who can't train themselves not to hear the screams." He smiles and his eyes twinkle. "So far no one has opted to have the operation, and I still have a one hundred percent success rate getting the screams out of people's heads. You see, most of my patients automatically stop hearing the screams the moment I even *suggest* the operation."

I look down at Maggie curled up in my lap. "I—I guess Maggie is a lucky cat," I stammer.

Dr. Babbitt looks at his cat, then his eyes look deep into mine. "Yes, Maggie's a very lucky cat. Some owners just let their pets go crazy, not realizing that there are, shall we say, *options*."

I cringe, wondering if my mother is aware of Dr. Babbitt's options . . . and his "lucky" cat.

"If only they could find a way to put the trees out of their misery," I say. "I mean, they've tried everything from burning them down to poisoning them, but the trees just keep growing back—faster!"

"Yes," Dr. Babbitt agrees. He frowns, then gets up and goes to a window.

I pick up Maggie and let her crawl up and ride on my shoulder as I follow him.

"How long do you suppose it'll be before they get here?" Dr. Babbitt asks, looking out at the horizon.

"It took them less than a year to cross Nebraska," I tell him. "And at the rate they're sprouting up and coming across Iowa they should reach Mortonville within a few weeks."

He nods, and glancing at me sideways, he opens the window. I guess he's trying to see if I will react, if I will cover my ears and run from the room like a mad person. I know what he's up to, and I do everything in my power to control myself, to *not* hear the screams of the trees.

Across the prairie, Dr. Babbitt and I can see the forest slowly advancing from one end of the horizon to the other. He picks up a pair of binoculars lying on the window sill and watches for a minute, then he passes them to me. In the distance I can see what remains of the town of Kittleton Springs, now swallowed up by trees. Lowering my line of sight, I study the edge of the forest. New saplings are sprouting and growing bigger as I watch.

"Such a strange sight," Dr. Babbitt comments.

I hand him the binoculars and cradle Maggie in my arms. Together, Dr. Babbitt and I watch the trees and listen to the screaming as they grow and grow and grow.

"So, Rebecca!" Dr. Babbitt yells over the screaming coming from outside the window, the screaming we both know I can hear. "Do you hear any screaming trees?"

Like I imagine all of his other patients did, patients who now claim to no longer hear the screaming, I yell back, "No, Dr. Babbitt! It's a miracle, but I can't hear them anymore!"

In my arms, Maggie yawns. She looks at her master, then rolls her head back and looks at me, wondering what we're making such a fuss about. And then, thankfully, Dr. Babbitt closes the window.

FUTURE CALLER

Kasi Shane's dad came into her room, putting on his polyurethane mask to cover his radiation scars. "I'm off to work," he said, his voice sounding slightly muffled behind the mask. "Now please, Kasi, no messing around with the PastPhone prototype. I don't want you in my lab anymore. Do you hear me?"

"Sure, Dad," said Kasi, lying on her lounge-bed, playing with a ringlet of her long auburn hair.

Her dad smiled under his mask. "See you around six," he said. And with a backward wave, he headed down the cell-hall.

"See ya, Dad!" called Kasi as she hit the multi-remote, closing her bedroom door. Then she listened as a hydro-taxi throttled down outside the dock by their house, and whisked her dad off to work.

Moments later, Kasi leaped off her lounge-bed with a mischievous grin, pressed the button on her room elevator, and was soon rising to her dad's lab on the third floor. She was sorry to be disobeying her father, but he just *had* to understand how bored she was. Anyway, she'd been careless the last time she'd used the PastPhone and left it ringing off the hook. She wouldn't make that mistake again.

It was no surprise to Kasi that her dad had left the outer door to his office open but had changed the access code on the electra-door into the main lab. "Poor Daddy. You're always trying to stay one step ahead of me," Kasi muttered, chuckling to herself. "But you don't really believe changing the code will do any good, do you? You forget, dear old Dad— you're dealing with the daughter of a genius."

A whiz with numbers, just like her father, Kasi deciphered the new code in just under thirty minutes, and soon she was walking around the messy lab shaking her head. "Whew, you may be a genius, Dad," she said, stepping over piles of paper on her way to the module that housed the PastPhone, "but you're also quite a slob!"

After carefully moving aside a stack of files from the chair in front of the PastPhone, Kasi settled down at the monitor and booted up the computer. Then she quickly punched in the password, **ALEX·G·BEL**, and smiled as the screen lit up a bright crimson red. She picked up the receiver and dialed a phone number at random . . . into the past.

"I'll get it!" Alicia Garcia called, putting her social studies book on the coffee table, and heading to the hall to grab the phone.

"Good, cuz I won't!" yelled her bratty little brother, Bernie, from the kitchen, his mouth full.

After saying a timid hello, Alicia was disappointed to hear a girl's voice on the other end of the line. She had been hoping for a call from Freddie Banks, her semi-boyfriend. But no such luck. Not only wasn't it Freddie, but it was some weird girl she didn't know who was talking nonsense.

"Please listen," said the distant voice on the other end of the line. "My name is Kasi Shane. Now I know it's going to be hard for you to believe this, but I'm calling from the future—from the year 3001."

"Well, you're wrong," replied Alicia sarcastically. "It's not *hard* for me to believe that at all—it's easy for me *not* to believe it. Now, if you'll excuse me, I—"

"Just listen to me," Kasi pleaded. "My father is a scientist, and he invented Bandwidth Telemetry. That's the basis of the PastPhone, which is what I'm talking to you on right now. Because of my dad's invention, a lot of people in your time period will soon be getting calls from people like me—people in the future, that is."

"What in the world are you talking about?" asked Alicia, getting annoyed. "Look, I'm going to hang up now. I'm expecting a phone call from the present."

"Please—don't hang up!" Kasi insisted and once again launched into an explanation of her father's invention.

"Get real," sneered Alicia. "And get a life!" With that she banged down the receiver.

"Who was on the phone?" asked Bernie, sauntering through the family room on his way out the back door.

"Just a crank call," Alicia said.

"Too bad it wasn't lover boy Fred-dee-pie!" Bernie teased, slamming the door before Alicia could say anything.

Frowning, Alicia picked up her textbook and was about to start studying again when the phone rang a second time.

"Please listen to me!" said the same voice on the other end of the line. "Please! I just need a friend to talk to!"

The girl sounded so desperate that Alicia kept the phone to her ear. "Go on," she said with a sigh. "I'm listening."

"What year have I reached?" asked Kasi.

Rolling her eyes, Alicia told her.

"Now tell me your name, age, and where you live," Kasi said. "If you tell me, I think I can prove to you that I'm telling the truth."

Alicia thought for a moment. Did she really want to give this crackpot all that information about herself? Still, the girl just sounded like she was lonely. What harm could it do? "Okay," she said. "My name is Alicia Garcia. I'm fourteen, and I live in Boulder, Colorado." She frowned. "So, prove to me you're calling from the future. I mean, you don't expect me to actually believe that baloney, do you?"

"I don't even understand exactly how my dad's invention works myself," said Kasi, "but I'm using a cellular telemetry phone that bridges not only space, but time. Honest, I'm not playing around."

"Keep talking," said Alicia, her skepticism turning to genuine curiosity.

"I live in what is approximately a thousand years into the future," said Kasi. "A thousand years into *your* future—in what used to be called Colorado but is now called the Greater Colorado Islands. Most of the United States is made up of islands now, because of the rains."

"What do you mean by 'the rains'?" Alicia asked.

"I've been told," said Kasi, "that it used to rain only once in a while. But because there's almost no more ozone layer, now it pours all the time. In fact, oceans cover most of the world—all but three percent of it."

"Wow!" Alicia exclaimed. If this girl was making this all up, she sure had a great imagination. "Tell me more, Kasi," she said eagerly.

"All the buildings—including my house—are tall, plasti-concrete structures, kind of like waterproof boxes on steel stilts," Kasi continued. "And everything is connected by canals. Anyway, there isn't much to do where I live, and there aren't many kids around because it's so hard to have a baby these days." She paused. "You see, radioactivity mutated a lot of women's reproductive systems, so now almost everyone is conceived in a test tube."

"You mean you were a test-tube baby?" asked Alicia.

"Yes, and both my parents were, too." Kasi was silent for a moment. "But my mom doesn't live with us anymore."

"Oh, I'm sorry," Alicia said. "Are your parents divorced?"

"Uh, not exactly," Kasi began. "My mom's skin couldn't handle the radiation levels above ground, so she had to move to one of the underground communities. Everybody develops radiation rashes and hardening of the skin when they grow up, and some people like my mom become too sensitive to live above ground."

"Gosh, that's terrible!" Alicia gasped.

"Yeah, it is," Kasi agreed. "And what makes it worse is my dad makes me stay indoors most of the time to protect my skin as much as possible." She sighed heavily. "It sure gets boring being cooped up day after day."

"Don't you have any friends?" Alicia asked sympathetically.

"A few, but there are less than a hundred and seventy kids in the Greater Colorado Island group, and the few I know I don't get to see very often. It's kind of hard getting around if you don't have a water-travel license, which I won't be able to get until I'm eighteen."

"How come the Earth is so messed up?" asked Alicia, totally fascinated.

"Like I said, the radioactivity," said Kasi. "There was quite a bit of fallout during World War Seven. But the real problem was the radioactive waste and molecular discharge from nuclear power plants that polluted the water and the atmosphere."

"Sounds awful," said Alicia.

"What's your world like?" asked Kasi. "Is it like they say it was in our history books?"

"I don't know what your books say," replied Alicia, "but it seems my world is—or should I say *was*—a lot nicer than yours."

"Tell me about your world," Kasi coaxed. "Please tell me everything you can think of!"

"Well, I live with my mom and stepdad and my goofy brother, Bernie. He's seven. Anyway, I go to Redland Middle School, and I'm just about the tallest girl in my class—which I hate." Alicia shrugged. "Other than that, I guess I'm just an average kid with sort of an average life."

"I wish I could meet you," said Kasi. "You sound nice." She hesitated. "Can I call you again?"

"Sure, I guess," said Alicia, deciding that whether or not Kasi was a legitimate caller from the future, she was still fun to talk to. "We can be sort of like pen pals who talk on a phone instead of using a pen."

"I've never used a pen," said Kasi. "I've seen pictures of them, but they're obsolete now since everything is done on computer."

"How cool!" exclaimed Alicia. "I'm going to love learning about the future!"

They began talking almost daily. Every now and then Alicia would wonder if it was all just some crazy joke being played on her, but little by little her doubts disappeared. In their place were feelings of wonderment and warmth for her new friend.

Alicia was keenly interested in everything Kasi had to say, and Kasi was just as fascinated with every aspect of Alicia's life. Usually the girls talked about ordinary things, but often they spoke about their feelings. Kasi described how lonely she felt because of her isolation, and Alicia talked a lot about being shy and wanting a steady boyfriend. Alicia also told Kasi about what she went through when her dad—her *real* dad—died, and about how hard it was when her mom remarried.

"How did your real dad die?" Kasi asked cautiously, not wanting to upset Alicia.

"Lung cancer," said Alicia. "He smoked cigarettes."

"I've read about cigarettes," said Kasi, "and I even saw some in a museum once." She paused. "It's so strange that people ever did that to themselves."

Alicia was about to respond when an idea suddenly hit her. "You know something, Kasi," she said. "If you live so far into the future, then in your time period I'm already dead."

"That's a scary thought," Kasi muttered.

"And you know what?" Alicia continued excitedly. "Since you live in the future, you can find out when I died . . . *and* how it happened."

"I guess I could," Kasi replied, growing a little uncomfortable. "But do you think that's something you really want to know?"

"Sort of," said Alicia. "I mean, it *is* a frightening thought, but it would be awfully interesting. And besides, maybe you could actually save my life!"

"You mean—?"

"Yeah, if I know in advance how I'm going to die, maybe I can prevent my own death!"

"Well," said Kasi, "looking at it in that way, yeah, of course I'll do it. I'll see what I can find out and call you tomorrow."

Using her dad's Batch Computation FORTRAN 8000 computer, Kasi was able to access the mainline biographics system in the Capitol Archives in Greater Appalachia, D.C. By punching in Alicia's name and date of birth, she was able to get a coded bio-read on her friend within minutes. But as she eagerly scanned the computer printout, a feeling of horror swept through Kasi. *Did I decode the information correctly?* she wondered. *And if I did, how can I tell Alicia what this says?*

Deciding that lying was her only option, Kasi made up a big story about how all the records referring to the year of Alicia's birth were destroyed by some kind of cosmic computer glitch. But she didn't even get halfway through her phony story before Alicia sensed something was wrong.

"Tell me," she begged. "I know you found out something. I can hear it in your voice."

Kasi took a deep breath. "I found out that you're going to die two days from now, on November 22nd, at 11:05 P.M.," she blurted. "It's because of a plane crash on the way to Las Vegas."

Alicia gasped. "My family and I are scheduled to fly to Las Vegas in two days to visit relatives for Thanksgiving . . . and our flight time would put us in the air at 11:05!"

"Then you've got to change everything," said Kasi. "Can you talk your family out of going, or maybe refuse to go?"

"No way. We're going for Thanksgiving," Alicia said, her voice shaky.

"Then how about changing your flight?" Kasi suggested.

"But what reason can I give?" Alicia asked. "The only thing I've told my family about you is that you're a new friend named Kasi. I never told them that you're from the future!"

"Then tell them," Kasi said. "Maybe they'll believe you."

"How could I tell them *that*? They'll think I've lost my mind!" Alicia practically yelled, wondering if she hadn't already gone crazy.

Kasi could hear the panic in Alicia's voice, but there was one more thing she had to tell her friend. "Look, Alicia," she said as calmly as she could. "I don't want to get you any more upset than you already are, but I looked up the names of the rest of your family, too, and they also die in the crash."

Alicia gasped. Now she *had* to try to change the future.

Frantically tossing ideas back and forth with her thirty-first century friend, Alicia suddenly had a brainstorm. "My stepdad is cheap!" she blurted out excitedly. "He wanted to drive in the first place, but I talked him into flying. What if I told him I realized how selfish I was being and that now I think we should go by car? I think he'll jump at the chance to save money!"

"You're a genius!" Kasi shouted. "What a great idea!"

Alicia's stepfather was surprised by her sudden change of heart, but as she'd predicted, he was delighted to save the airfare. In fact, he was going to borrow a friend's motor home so they wouldn't have to pay for restaurants or motel rooms either.

"The plan worked perfectly," Alicia told Kasi the next day. "The way my stepdad figures it, we can still leave tomorrow and get there on time for Thanksgiving."

"That's great, Alicia," Kasi said with relief. "I'll call you when you get back."

At the crack of dawn on November 22, Alicia and her family headed off in the motor home to Las Vegas. Everybody was in a good mood. None of them had ever gone anywhere in a motor home before, and it was fun to be able to move around, play board games, and even stretch out for a nap.

Alicia felt relieved as they whisked along the highway, but still a little apprehensive as the afternoon wore on. After dinner she decided to lie down on one of the fold-out beds to relax, and she soon drifted into a troubled sleep. She dreamed she was in a crowded airplane miles above the ground, when suddenly she heard a loud explosion. Then she felt herself falling through the air and saw the ground rushing up at her.

After waking with a start, Alicia heaved a sigh of relief when she felt the calming rumble of the motor home as they sped smoothly along the highway. She sat up and, looking out the window, she saw nothing but an endless dark highway surrounded by desert.

"Have a nice sleep?" asked her mom, looking over her shoulder from the front passenger seat. "You've been conked out for hours!"

"You were snoring like a bear," Bernie said with an annoying giggle.

Alicia rolled her eyes and went back to looking out the window at the black landscape whizzing by. Then she looked at her digital watch. It was already ten minutes to eleven. Only fifteen minutes away from the time that Kasi said she was supposed to die. Even though they weren't in an airplane, a chill went down her spine.

"Even Mom said you were snoring a little," said Bernie, poking Alicia in the side. "Just like a grizzly!"

Alicia ignored him, her eyes fixed on her watch. Slowly the numbers flipped forward—10:52 . . . 10:53 . . . 10:54 . . .

"Want to play checkers?" asked Bernie, trying a new tactic to get his sister's attention.

"No!" Alicia almost shouted, her body tense.

"What's your problem?" he asked, looking hurt. "I was trying to be nice."

Turning away from Bernie, Alicia put her hand over her watch and stared out the window. *I'm not even going to look at the time*, she told herself, wishing she could somehow talk to Kasi.

An eternity seemed to pass. Finally, unable to resist the temptation, Alicia lifted her hand and looked at her watch again. It was 11:04. Wanting to throw her watch out the window, she continued to stare at it until the number flipped over to 11:05! Her heart racing, Alicia kept staring at her watch, willing it to pass the time of her death . . . and then . . . it was 11:06.

Nothing happened! her mind screamed. Sagging back into her seat, Alicia smiled with relief. She and Kasi had done it. Together they had managed to change the future!

In the front seat, her mom and stepdad started talking about stopping for the night.

"It's getting late," said her mom. "Everybody start looking for a rest stop."

Her stepdad yawned, then turned on the radio. "Sounds good to me," he said. "I've got about an hour's driving left in me, and then I'm ready to turn in."

"Where are we?" asked Bernie.

"Nevada," said his mother.

Feeling good, Alicia gazed out the window as the motor home droned along the dark highway for the next hour. She kept thinking how happy Kasi would be that together they had managed to avert disaster.

Ahead was a cluster of lights.

"That's Mesa Blanca," said her stepdad. "And if I remember correctly, there's a rest stop just a few miles up the road."

The song playing on the radio came to an end and was replaced by the voice of a DJ. "This is Larry Lee on K-LOV, and it's 11:04 on a very lovely Nevada night."

The hair stood up on the back of Alicia's neck. "How come that DJ said it's 11:04?" she almost shouted, staring at her watch. "It's 12:04!"

"We passed from Mountain Standard Time to Pacific Standard Time while you were asleep," said her mom. "There's a one-hour time difference."

"You forgot to set your stupid watch back," Bernie said with a laugh.

"It's still Wednesday!" gasped Alicia. "And in a few seconds it's going to be—"

But no one could hear the rest of Alicia's sentence over the horrid roar that filled the night. Then they saw the lighted mass of a crippled 747 as it tried to make an emergency landing on the highway. The huge wheels of the jet squealed as they touched down on the asphalt, and for a split second Alicia saw the anguished face of the pilot in the cockpit window. She and her family barely had time to scream as the massive jet plowed through them, instantly making them a part of the past.

Four days later, Kasi Shane dialed Alicia's number. More than a thousand years in the past, a phone rang in an empty house. "What went wrong?" she cried. "We had it all figured out!" Kasi frantically dialed the number again, hoping she'd misdialed the first time, but the phone just continued to ring and ring and ring. . . .